Learning to Heel

By Lynne E. Scott

*For Douglas,
Kayla + Hudson ~
Many blessings,
Lynne '15*

Copyright © 2015 Lynne E. Scott
All rights reserved.
ISBN-10: 1519135289
ISBN-13: 978-1519135285

"One does not love a place the less for having suffered in it unless it has all been suffering, nothing but suffering."
Jane Austen

"We live, in fact, in a world starved for solitude, silence and privacy; and therefore starved for meditation and true friendship."
C.S. Lewis

*"Where is the heart that does not keep
Within its inmost core
Some fond remembrance hidden deep
Of days that are no more?"*
Ellen Clementine Howarth

Chapter One–A Broken Spirit

"You can never take the spark out of Sparky. Being obedient doesn't mean he will lose his essence," she told the dog owners, their six month old large mixed breed tugging at the end of its leash. He sniffed all around the porch and lunged for a cat sitting on top of a fence post a short distance away.

Lauren often avoided errands in her small town whenever possible. As the local dog trainer, even the simplest errand may run long if someone had a question or stopped to tell her a story. But this was new. She'd never had people show up at her door unannounced with an unruly dog in tow. Fortunately she was used to her privacy being interrupted. And clearly they were desperate for answers.

Wendy, Sparky's owner, struggled to keep him away from Lauren's dogs who sat quietly watching from inside. "At home he's awful too. He stole a pork chop off the table when I turned my back for a second!"

"We've had him six weeks and he's ripped up a lot of my clothes," her husband, Martin, added. At the sound of his voice, Sparky turned his attention toward Martin and jumped with front paws outstretched.

Wendy whispered, "Sparky chewed up his underwear!"

"Why did you whisper? There's no one else around here!" her husband said good-naturedly. "Lauren's out in the middle of nowhere."

Lauren smiled. Being far out in the country was more than just the physical location of her home and training facility. Some days she felt just as isolated on the inside. "Keep in mind that I train owners to train their dogs. It's you who have to do the hard work."

Wendy shook her head, "I hate to give him up, but he's driving us crazy."

Lauren motioned for the leash and took it, jogging away so that Sparky followed. She stopped, keeping her eyes off the dog, while Sparky ran past her and stopped short at the end of the leash. The dog gave a sharp yelp, as did Wendy. Quickly Lauren dashed at an angle, the dog trying to keep up. Again she stopped and the dog raced by with the same result of an abrupt stop. After a few more sharp turns, the dog's attention was on Lauren.

"He's a smart pup. You really should consider taking him through obedience classes. I want you to keep him for the rest of his life, but it sounds like he needs to learn a few things."

"You're sure you won't break his spirit?" Wendy fussed as she took Sparky's leash back only to have the dog spring toward her nose.

Lauren smirked. She was used to whining and whimpering in obedience classes. It didn't all come from the dogs.

"Obedience training is to motivate a dog to behave in a more controlled and consistent manner so he can be a good member of your home. Keep in mind we train children as they grow for the same purpose, and it's not to break them down into robots."

"When's your next class begin?" Martin asked seizing the leash from his wife and putting the dog into the crate in the back of his pickup.

"Just two weeks," Lauren handed him a list of classes which he examined as he climbed into the driver's seat.

Wendy gently grabbed Lauren's arm, "How are you getting along, Lauren? I mean, I know it's been a year, but I just don't know how you could ever get over losing someone as great as Tyler."

Irritation flared in Lauren, but years of forcing herself to be polite took over, "That's very kind of you."

After the couple and their exuberant dog left, Lauren wondered why anyone would think she would be involved with dog obedience if it was actually harmful to dogs. Sometimes it seemed everyone questioned her judgment, yet somehow she managed to run her business while suffering some of the worst stress of her life without falling apart. Of course, Wendy was one of her friends who managed to make herself scarce when things with Tyler became more difficult.

Although a lot of work, the dogs forced her to function and get out of bed every morning. Having them depend on her kept her from brooding. The obedience classes often helped more than just the owner train their dog to be a civilized member of the household. Sometimes Lauren found herself using the principles to adapt her own behavior.

She thought about what she'd told Wendy and Martin. She hoped they would trust her advice. Lauren didn't always trust others either. It's easy to follow when there's trust. But when life has been painful, it's hard to believe.

Over the last decade, she'd watched her healthy husband's muscles deteriorate under the ravages of ALS. It took so much of him, but never his essence. Tyler's happy spirit never broke as their lives changed from one of promise to one of waiting. Now, Lauren had come to terms with the pain, it was building a life from here that seemed to have unpredictable obstacles.

If stress aged a person, she was much older than her thirty-six years.

*

"You're good looking, but not that good looking."

"What's that supposed to mean?" Michael glared at Kelly, whose legs were over the back of the couch and the rest of her body lounged at an awkward angle. She fidgeted with her hair. Michael was impatient when she fidgeted, which was any time she had an arbitrary thought.

"Like, I seen pictures of you in those early movies."

Michael winced, not only because of Kelly's poor command of English grammar but he sensed what she was going to say next.

"Where's that Starbucks where them paparazzi wait to film

stars?" Kelly asked.

"You mean 'where those' not 'where them.' I've told you before–rule number one is to speak properly," Michael hoped his tone was helpful and didn't reveal how this grated on his nerves.

Kelly huffed, "What are you, some kind of teacher? No one cares about that stuff no more. Now where is it?"

Michael sensed the demand behind her question. "We live two doors down from a perfectly good coffee house."

Kelly rolled her eyes, "As if. It's not like I'm after actual coffee, Captain Obvious." Kelly's lap dog, Buttons, hopped onto the couch next to her.

"Could you please keep the dog off the couch? I don't want to keep picking fine dog hair from my jeans."

Kelly scooped the dog into her arms, not moving him. She shot Michael a look, "What I'm trying to say is that you were real cute and it made sense you were the teen heartthrob."

"Now I'm not a heartthrob?" Michael looked at her, pressing the fingertips of his hands together. "Then why are you with me?"

"No, Mickey, it's just that then you sort of were equal with the other teens."

Michael got up and poured himself a half shot of whiskey and soda. "Please stop talking."

Kelly shrugged and snapped on the television, indulging in her main fare of gossip programs that reported on celebrities famous for accomplishing nothing. Michael called them hollow. Kelly called it research.

As Michael stirred his drink, he noticed his hand shook ever so much. He didn't want to admit how far on edge he felt, but here was proof that maybe it was worse than he expected. While Kelly lacked depth and wasn't much for meaningful conversation, what she said hit a nerve. She might be right. And if the current movie didn't do at least moderately well . . . he didn't want to think about that.

The movie industry was cruel. He was fortunate that as a teen his early movies were successful, many a part of a new director's popular body of work. At the time, he was proud of that. When he hit his late twenties, he found he wanted to distance himself from what was sometimes an embarrassing gap in momentum as reviewers were not always kind in his role selection.

Smugly, he began to choose roles in what he considered "films" not movies. They tanked like the Titanic—not the movie success of *Titanic,* but the actual sunk-to-the-depths ship. His agent pressured him into taking some high action films as the second lead. Humiliated, he accepted, and happily his talent was commended, even though it was for a movie that Michael thought was trite. He was no longer a heartthrob. He wasn't an action hero. What was he? Who could he trust to determine the answer?

Now, as age forty loomed, his challenge was more difficult. With a constant pool of hungry, aggressive actors chasing his heels, romantic comedy leads were no longer offered. If he didn't find something soon, the part of "supporting actor" would become his only choice. Kelly's words finalized his worst fears that she and Hollywood both believed the worst–he was not aging well.

Quickly he added another full shot to his drink. Who was he fooling? And what was he doing with Kelly? She didn't care about the craft of acting. And, according to some gossips, she was too young for him, as if he was using her.

If they only knew. Kelly's cunning mind attracted him the first time they met, despite her poor grasp of grammar. It didn't hurt that she was also beautiful. Beauty was easy to find in his circles. Cleverness was not. But after six months of being together, it seemed that her ways were more conniving than smart. He seemed more a part of her plan than a part of a relationship.

"We're still going to the thing tonight, right?" Kelly's voice had a decidedly firm tone. She wasn't asking him. She was telling him her plan.

"You know I hate those premieres," Michael laid on the opposite sofa, his face away from the television. He did hate them. But he needed them. He hated that he needed them. He was never sure if it was the recognition for his work or just the recognition that was his addiction.

"Listen, you promised we'd go. It's good for you to be seen since you're working on something now." Kelly pouted. "Besides, you will love the dress I picked for it."

"It's good for you to be seen too, isn't it Kelly?" He put his emptied drink on the coffee table and put a pillow over his face.

"Of course it is. And we're going. So take your old man nap and then get dressed."

As he closed his eyes, he wondered who was actually the one being manipulated. Fortunately, he drifted off to sleep, ocean sounds from his open sliding glass door lulling him.

*

"The cat condo gave you a black eye?" Alice's crossed arms reinforced her disbelief in Lauren's story. "Have you been drinking that Florida hot chocolate again?"

Lauren sighed. "Honestly, it's your fault. You and Tish are the ones who decided to rearrange the furniture. I got up in the middle of the night and I walked right into the second story platform."

Alice examined Lauren's eye. "Yeah, you're going to have a shiner. If you had fewer cats, you wouldn't need that unsightly cat furniture."

"What am I supposed to do? They get dumped here. The shelters are full," Lauren batted the catnip mouse on the spring, luring her gray cat to hop up and begin playing. "Tyler is the one who said that any creature who sets foot on this property was sent for a reason. I'm just giving them a chance for life."

"I know, and that's admirable, but you can't save them all." Alice softened. "It's expensive, for one thing. Besides, you're running out of names. You're calling them after root vegetables. What kind of a name is Parsnip?"

"Why did you have to move everything around anyway?" Lauren muttered, catching herself as she almost sat where a chair used to be. She glared at Alice as she took a couple steps to the chair's new spot, frowning as she sank into it.

Alice walked to the sofa's new location and sat on its arm. "I know you really enjoy your early garage sale décor, but we wanted to freshen the place up, add a few things—"

"Take away even more." Lauren snapped.

"Yeah, but did you really need the horse lamp?"

Lauren shifted her eyes away. "I've stubbed my toe twice."

"And a chair made out of belts?" Alice pressed. "And the tennis racket picture frame?"

"Tyler really enjoyed upcycling."

A long silence punctuated the air.

Finally, Alice crossed back to Lauren and knelt beside her, "We moved the furniture because it was time, Lauren. It's time for you to move on too."

"I just had Wendy on me and now you." Lauren rolled her eyes and shot up from the chair, "Has it occurred to anyone that maybe I'm the best judge of when it's time to move on? And what does that even mean?" Lauren shifted the chair back to its previous location. "When Tyler was sick, the furniture was out of the way of his wheelchair. I'm used to seeing it like this. There have been enough adjustments. Right now, my house floor plan isn't going to be one more."

Alice shrugged and followed Lauren into the kitchen where filled coffee cups were waiting. "You know it's just that we want your life to be fulfilling."

Lauren softened, "My life is fulfilling. You're looking out for me and I do appreciate that. Now, if only I could explain to Franny Bottoms that I don't need her to keep bringing me casseroles."

Alice whipped around to face Lauren, "She still brings those things?"

Lauren nodded her head slowly, "You bet. Doesn't miss a week of delivering one of her rather frightening casseroles. Honestly, it's like she doesn't know one person lives here."

"Maybe she knows you don't go to the grocery store," Alice smirked. "You know neither Tish nor I mind doing it, but isn't it time to get back out there?"

Lauren wrapped her hands around her coffee mug, "With Tish on her honeymoon, it's fallen on you. That's not fair." She grinned at her friend, "But it's so much easier to stay away."

Alice snorted, "Lauren, when have you shied away from doing difficult things? And shopping isn't hard. You can interact with the public. You've continued with your dog boarding business and the obedience training classes all through Tyler's illness."

"That's different. The grocery store brings back a lot of memories–Ty's favorite food, the snacks we had while watching movies. Besides, with the kennel it's my turf–my house, my rules." Lauren got back up for a refill. "I went to church once since Tyler's death. I tried to sneak in but I ended up in the back row where all the old widows sit. I can't say I'm comfortable with my peer group yet. And then the usher gave me that sappy look."

"They mean well too. You can't be too hard on them. No one knows the right way to act or what to say."

Lauren shook her head defiantly, "I don't know about that. When I did the whole peace hand shake thing with Wendy's husband, she glared at me like I'm out to steal him from her. That's sure not meaning well."

"Has it occurred to you that the longer you wait, the worse it gets built up in your mind? Get out there–do some errands, go back to your book club and other groups. For Pete's sake, update your phone!" Alice often was overly exuberant when she tried to give a pep talk.

Lauren laughed, "You are telling me to update my phone? You don't even e-mail! Besides, I like my little flip phone. A widow shouldn't have anything too flashy."

Alice grabbed Lauren's hand, "Stop it. Stop playing the widow card. You've been known as Tyler's wife. But you are more than that. Do you hear me? Now start acting like it."

*

"Mickey, would it kill you to dress up now and then? You look like the bums one street over." Kelly hissed her disgust at him.

Michael looked at his attire. Anything would pass in Hollywood. "I can't believe you talked me into coming to Blake Greer's premiere." Michael said.

"Just think of the free publicity."

Michael paused with her and mumbled, "It's one thing I

dread."

"It's one thing I need," Kelly said so quietly that even Michael didn't hear her.

Kelly looped her arm through his, pausing now and then so her legs would show to their best display, flashing her perfect, chemically enhanced smile. It was apparent that she knew her striking beauty brought attention to Michael, who likely wouldn't get much on his own.

As the couple inched their way down the path to the theater, Michael watched as the majority of the crowd looked past him, trying to find someone more important. It was something he noticed more and more and he didn't want to admit how much it bothered him. He also noticed how so many people just held up their phones, watching through the screen instead of the live action. How strange technology made the world seem in just the couple of decades he'd been in acting.

"Alright, Kelly, rule number five, never look desperate for attention. Let them come to you," Michael smoothed back his hair.

A very attractive young woman looked him dead in the eye and waved her perfectly toned arm at him. Normally he tried to avoid direct contact. But she was hard to resist and he slipped out of Kelly's grasp while she preened for some photographers.

Michael said hello and leaned in close to the girl for a picture. She pulled back and gave him a strange look, "What are you doing?" She pushed an older woman next to him. "My mom says she practically grew up with you. Smile, Mom!"

The older woman smiled enthusiastically while Michael plastered his celebrity grin onto his face. He couldn't help but wonder if this picture was going to look as fake and awkward as it felt when it no doubt was plastered over the woman's social media accounts.

The young woman said, "Okay, that was great." She didn't pull her phone away though. The next thing he knew, the mom grabbed his face and kissed him full on the lips. It was impossible for him to hide his surprise and the daughter's laughter confirmed it. As the mother scampered back in the crowd, he noticed the daughter finally stopped filming the incident. "See ya on YouTube!" she said.

Michael felt sick. It wasn't so much that he'd been forced to kiss an older woman, or that he was even remotely as old as her, though neither made him feel good about himself. What bothered him most was that neither cared what they'd done.

His stomach churned. For the first time in months, he looked around actually wanting Kelly's company. At least she was a temporary refuge from the complexities of his world. Most of the time, anyway.

Kelly found him first and drug him to the spot where one of the so called "entertainment" shows was broadcasting. Michael recognized the show host, Chet Davis, just as he motioned to him to step up to the small platform. Kelly again nudged him and forward they went.

"Mick Quinlan! It's great to see you out on the town tonight. Who's this hottie with you?"

Michael put his arm around Kelly's shoulders to bring her

closer to the camera, "This is the one and only Kelly Smith."

Feeling a jab from Kelly's pointy elbow, he realized his mistake, "Fairbanks. This is Kelly Fairbanks, the up and coming model you've probably seen so much of lately."

Kelly leaned in and assumed a sudden air of sophisticated cool, "Love your show, Chet."

Just then a wave of hysteria moved through the crowd. Chet turned to the camera, "That can mean only one thing. Blake Greer is in the house!" Pandemonium broke out and Michael and Kelly stared at Chet's back. The camera panned the crowd and Chet turned for the briefest of moments to dismiss them, "Thanks, Mick, Pam."

He rushed away with Kelly yelling after him, "It's Kelly! Kelly!"

Kelly looked at Michael with serious disappointment. He felt unusually protective of her. He remembered the first time he took his first brutal lessons in the celebrity world. As they walked away, he looked at her and said, "Lesson Six: When you're not the man of the hour, you're nobody."

Chapter Two–The Trusted Friend

"What is the first lesson in dog obedience?" Lauren Sanders asked the circle of dog owners. It was the first day of a new session of classes. The ten owners and their dogs varied in age, breed and temperament. And at this moment, confusion also reigned as they offered their guesses.

"Sit?"

"Come?"

"Stop eating my socks?" the owner of a Labrador asked.

The group laughed, Lauren grinned, "Those are all good answers, and we'll get to all of those eventually. What you may call 'stop eating my socks' we call 'drop it.' Or, if you're not careful, 'emergency vet visit.'"

"Oh, we've already gone that route. That's why I want to learn it right away," the man said. "Good thing I bought pet insurance!"

Lauren patted the head of the Labrador before walking to

the center of the group, "Let me ask you a different question. When someone tells you to do something, how do you react?"

"With hostility," the poodle owner said.

"Okay, I can relate to where you're coming from! Anyone else?" Lauren worked the room with confidence. Though she was shy, it was easy to feel in charge when she was talking about something she understood well.

"I do it–it's easier than fighting," the owner of a Bernese mountain dog said.

Lauren glanced at the dog, "Is that how your dog reacts to you?"

The owner reddened, "Not at all. That's why we're here."

"It depends on who it is," the Lab owner replied.

Lauren turned to look at him. "To whom will you listen?"

"My wife, of course. I am not a stupid man!"

Lauren struggled to keep from laughing, "And you listen to your wife because you trust her, I assume?"

The man nodded.

"So the answer is that we respond positively to someone we trust. Today we'll talk about what builds trust and what can destroy it." Lauren took the leash from the poodle who was winning the war on leash chewing with its owner. She walked quickly from one end of the circle to the other as she talked. As soon as she stopped, the dog tried to take the leash in its mouth. Before it could, Lauren walked quickly in the opposite direction.

"Most dog owners enjoy spoiling their dog to some extent, particularly when they are new to our home. Your dog happily accepts food from you, goes outside when it wants, and probably has manipulated you into playing with him when he's in the mood. If you're not careful, you may be seen as only an instrument for getting what the dog wants and not that you actually have any power."

The wife of the Lab owner cocked her head to the side and looked at her husband. The man raised his hand, "Guilty!"

"When your dog gets everything it wants out of life, there's no reason for it to trust you. It's only when you ask the dog to do something that he gets to decide whether you are worthy of his obedience." Lauren grinned. "You're here to prove you're worthy!"

The wife of the Lab owner shouted, "You're worthy, Honey!" He responded with an embarrassed thumbs up.

"Things that build trust: gentleness, firmness, structure. Things that destroy trust: abuse, fear, neglect." Lauren continued to move with the poodle, who now was watching Lauren, anticipating her movements and forgetting all about the leash.

The owner of a mixed breed spoke up, "My dog was abused before I got her. What am I supposed to do?" The dog tentatively watched the class from behind her owner's legs.

"I have an abused dog myself. It takes a long time to rebuild trust. Training is the way you do it. The most amazing thing about training is that not only does your dog learn to respond to what you ask of him, he learns to trust you."

"I was afraid it would make him more afraid if I was bossing him around."

"That's a common myth. However, a dog needs to follow someone. If you don't show him the way, he'll make up his own rules. As you might guess, generally the rules dogs come up with don't go well with living with human beings."

Lauren noticed that most of the class was now staring at the young poodle, including the dogs. She looked down at the dog and met her gaze, "What do you think, Georgianna? Do you trust me?"

The dog wagged the small puff of her tail and the class responded with giggles and even some applause.

"So you see that showing a dog a better way to live isn't an exercise in brutality and force. It is simply a matter of getting the dog's attention like we've done just now and establishing trust."

After this Lauren put the class through their own paces having them walk in a circle as the dogs followed or attempted to go their own way. "Don't wait for your dog. If he's lagging behind, walk faster. Then he has to keep up with you—to pursue you." The owner of the Bernese was at a near sprint to maintain her dog's attention.

By the end of class everyone was tired, but the smiles on the owners' faces and the lolling tongues of the dogs revealed that it was that good kind of tired that resulted from learning and doing at the same time. Lauren handed out some papers with the homework for the owners and dogs to work on for the following week.

"Be sure to practice getting your dog's attention this week. You won't make good progress if you don't practice. We'll be moving along quickly, but we'll revisit all the other commands. These are building blocks."

The Labrador owner stopped, his wife by his side, "Do you think this mutt will ever listen to me?"

Lauren nodded, "Remember, you're worthy."

*

Michael asked Kelly to move in with him too soon. However, being tied to a moderately-high profile relationship was nearly as important as being tied to a film project. Without both, his clout was in jeopardy. What was maddening was clout could not be quantified, though social networks made valiant attempts to measure a person's relevance.

After two months of living with her, it was tough for him to decide if the ease of having someone to have sex with and water his plants was worth the aggravation Kelly gave him.

Generally, the frustration started early in the day. It wasn't enough that his day began with a careful examination of his aging skin in the mirror, wondering if a wrinkle formed overnight or if his nose was outgrowing his face. No, the messes Kelly left in the shower disgusted him.

"Could you please put the hair left in the shower drain in the trash pail instead of flinging it against the side of the shower wall?" Michael asked as he toweled off his hair. At least it wasn't thinning.

Kelly was sprawled on the couch, dressed as fashionably as

possible, complete with impractical shoes. She didn't bother to look up from her celebrity magazine. "Oh smell my butt."

Michael rolled his eyes, "It's your dignity and poise that I admire so much in you."

Kelly waved her hand at him, dismissing his opinion, engrossed in every detail of the magazine.

"By the way, next time you want to roll the red carpet, leave me out of it." Michael took his towel into the bathroom. "Three in one month is enough. I don't care if you like the growing attention. It's not good for you."

"Next time I won't need you," Kelly murmured, unheard by Michael.

When he came back out, he paused to watch as Kelly set down her magazine and examined her belly and breasts. Was her belly too big? Her breasts too small? He knew the picture of insecurity when he saw it. Over the decades of the celebrity factory, he saw it over and over. For a minute, he felt bad for her. He leaned over the couch to kiss her.

Kelly presented her cheek instead. Michael kissed it, and moved her chin gently so she'd look him in the eyes, "Rule number nine: don't let the media define who you are."

"Maybe you should write a manual with all your stupid rules. That might make some money," Kelly snorted.

"I don't know why I bother, you don't listen to me." Michael took the remote control from her side and clicked on the television.

Kelly sat up straight, "Turn on Star News. I want to see if Chet Davis runs that interview with me."

"What did I just say? That show will warp your self-image forever if you're not careful. Besides, the interview was with me."

Kelly leapt like a cat and snatched the remote from him, "Whatever." Knowing the station well, she flipped to it and watched as the host interviewed a beautiful older actress.

Michael leaned in, "That's Tanya Jenkins. We did a movie together years ago."

As he listened to the line of questioning of the host, Michael got a sense of where the conversation was going. Past lovers. It was fodder for every interview. And he knew Tanya well enough to know she liked to dish up gossip with anyone who asked.

"Give me that," Michael reached for the remote, but Kelly quickly slipped it under her body. Michael's thoughts were suddenly diverted and engaged with the game. Kelly giggled as Buttons yipped and nipped at Michael.

"All Mickey's talk about 'finding meaning' just got so tiresome. I mean, duh, we're living it, right?"

The words on the television from Tanya caused Buttons and Kelly to stop and watch. Michael heard too, but he refused to look. He cringed and sat on the edge of the couch instead, "Funny how I was good enough for her until she got an award winning script."

"Bitter old women write tell-alls. Look at all her wrinkles,"

Kelly said, her only thoughts on comforting. "High-def ain't kind to the elderly!"

Michael sighed, "We're the same age."

Getting up, Michael turned off the television when he walked by. Kelly turned it right back on with the remote. He turned to glare at her. She stuck out her tongue at him.

"What are you? Five years old?" Michael felt his temper rising. Normally, he kept his cool, but she was pushing him.

Kelly raised the volume and Chet Davis' voice filled the room, "Look at the turnout last night for Blake Greer's instant classic."

Michael turned to watch the footage, "There's no such thing as an 'instant classic.' "

"Shut up!" Kelly snapped.

He couldn't believe her tone. What was worse, he couldn't believe how focused she was on the show. Michael turned toward his television and regretted buying such a large screen. A wide shot showed just how packed the theater was, the red carpet a stream through an undulating crowd. Kelly cheered as a brief shot of her and Michael flashed. Then the high pitched squeals of the younger girls screaming Blake's name pierced the air as the camera zoomed in on the star of the hour.

"Wow, that was some crowd," Michael uttered.

"Yeah, it was great. They really loved me," Kelly agreed, but far from the sentiment Michael intended.

Michael turned the television off and glared. Kelly's eyes

grew big, "Hey, how about you propose to me? Then we'll break up in some staged fight at a restaurant. Imagine the headlines!"

"No way," Michael said. "I like to keep my fragile grip on reality."

She shrugged, "I think I'll start my own YouTube channel. I wonder what my signature look should be."

Kelly was lost to the real world. Another victim.

He grabbed a half bottle of water that sat on the coffee table and took a swig. He thought of the crowd that was cheering the latest name. He remembered what a rush it was when he first experienced it. That buoyed him for years. Now his screen time was more like a quaint gesture. He felt sick.

Maybe this sequel he was working on now would fare well. It had to. This life was all he knew.

He needed to get out and clear his head. Maybe a run on the beach. He had to stay in shape. He stood up and walked toward the kitchen. Along the way, he noticed that the fern by the porch was wilting with neglect. He poured what remained in the water bottle over it, hoping it could be saved.

*

When Tyler was still alive, every waking moment of Lauren's time was taken. With caring for the dogs in the kennel, obedience classes in the evenings, making meals, cleaning the house, Tyler's various needs—not to mention their own dogs and cats—the days were often a blur.

Now, she was still adjusting to the hours of free time. She remembered how Tyler told her that after he died, she'd probably sleep for a year. At the time, it seemed funny but it turned out to be close to the truth. As she sat on her back porch swing, she breathed in the warm air, glad she didn't need the afternoon naps anymore. For the last couple of weeks, the bullfrogs in the pond made plenty of noise. She watched as one of her cats stalked them.

Tyler insisted she sell their country home after he was gone, not wanting her to continue the hard work it demanded. Right now it was hard to imagine being anywhere else. Strangely, since her pace slowed considerably, she was enjoying the peace of it. No neighbors close by, setting her own schedule–those were the good points.

Besides, she had no idea what she'd do if she moved. Where would she go? How would she earn a living? It would be hard to put on a resumé what she'd been up to for the last ten years. She wondered if someone who was self-employed could write their own letter of recommendation.

She smiled at the thought. Then she remembered one of the last conversations she'd had with Tyler.

When she walked into the living room after doing the dishes, she noticed him writing on a large legal pad. His hand strength was limited and she knew his writing was awful. When he noticed her presence, he set it down with a mischievous grin.

"What are you up to now?" Lauren sat on the couch next to his lift-chair, trying to peak at the paper.

Tyler drew it toward him and wagged the pen at her, "I'm

working on your letter of recommendation."

"My what? Do you think that after the kennel I'm going to become a nurse's aide or something?"

Tyler thought a moment, "That wouldn't be a bad choice for you. You are awfully strong from wrestling those Rottweilers and carrying me around. But no, this is my recommendation of how great a wife you are."

Lauren felt something in her chest tighten, "I'm not following you."

"Someday you're going to meet a man who, while not as fabulous as me, might be a suitable husband for you. I'm leaving a letter of recommendation."

"Like I'm applying for a job?"

"Maybe it should be more of an instructor's manual." Lauren reached for the tablet but in an unusual moment of deftness, Tyler swatted her hand away. "See what I mean? The next guy needs to know what he's in for with you–the good and the bad."

Lauren crossed her arms, "The bad? You may want to watch what you say? I do feed you, you know."

Tyler acted as if he were making another note and mumbled, "Threatens the weak by withholding food."

Lauren laughed and leaned toward him, "Tyler, I'd rather keep the husband I've got."

Tyler set the tablet down and took Lauren's hand. "I'd rather you did too. But we've got reality staring us in the face so let's get on with it. Let me make this very clear, you choose a man who is willing to carry you and not the other way around. Got it?"

Lauren smiled, seeing the weary look in his eyes, which she likely had in her own. "Want me to make some popcorn before we watch the movie?"

"Sure," Tyler picked up the remote and surfed past some channels, settling on a cooking show. "Remember when Franny Bottoms brought me that first chicken casserole?"

Lauren frowned, "I try to block out that particular nightmare." She reached over and picked up Tyler's cane and put it in the umbrella rack.

Tyler changed the station to one with hikers on a mountain. "Remember when we took that cave tour the summer after we got married?"

Lauren looked back at the television and frowned. "Sort of."

"Sort of? I carried you back to the truck when you almost fainted with claustrophobia." Tyler looked at her with alarm. "Are you going to remember me at all?"

How could he have asked her such a thing? Still today, she hated that he worried about that. But she had little control over her time, let alone the luxury of reminiscing. At the time, she had no idea how close to death he was. After a few weeks of difficulties, things had calmed down. His breathing issues seemed pretty stable. If only she'd known these were his last days.

Lauren got up and headed to the kennel. She felt bitter, but she was determined to keep that at bay. It was too late to undo those days. What movie did they even watch that night? She was pretty sure it was an old Mick Quinlan movie. She and Tyler grew up watching his early films and always were entertained by them. It seemed like they couldn't get enough of comedy, needing to laugh and forget the reality all around them.

After situating the dogs in the outside runs, Lauren filled the water bowls. She looked around her at the kibble scattered across the floor along with some clumps of fur. There was a stack of dirty dog bowls in the corner that needed her attention. "Get with it, Sister." Lauren mumbled to herself.

She opened the back door and her dog Guinness swaggered in with two of the dogs she was caring for in the kennel. All three seemed happy and tired after a good play session. Each went to their kennel run voluntarily and began to lap at the water. "A tired dog is a good dog." Guinness cocked his head as if he were trying to understand her. "Here, let's put you in here while the others come in."

As she pointed at one of the empty wire cages, Guinness obediently entered. She heard barking turn aggressive in the outside areas. Quickly she darted out the door in time to see two dogs barking at each other. Fortunately chain link fence separated them. "Rocky, knock it off!" Lauren shouted. Rocky stopped and she lifted the latch to bring him inside. The dog looked over his shoulder one more time, "No! Leave it alone!" The dog followed her and she scolded him one more time, "Why must you make a fight where there is no fight?"

Lynne E. Scott

Chapter Three–Failure

"Wendy, don't be afraid to fail with Sparky," Lauren said into her phone as she walked onto her back porch. "You may be learning new skills right along with your dog. Don't be concerned that he doesn't know how to do everything at once. It's step by step. If you only get him to sit once today, that's a victory. You've only been at this a couple of weeks."

"He ripped up another pair of Martin's underwear!" Wendy yelled.

Lauren pulled the phone away from her ear as Wendy continued to list Sparky's offenses. Finding a break when Wendy took a breath, Lauren jumped in, "Bear with Sparky's mistakes. You'll make some too. But soon you'll both make fewer. Some failures are necessary so you can win later."

Dead silence met Lauren's words. Finally, Wendy took a deep breath, "I sure hope you're right."

After the call ended, Lauren shook her head. Some dog owners gave up because they didn't see immediate results. It was so hard to stress the patience required to train properly. Owners needed to trust the process.

Lauren looked over her back porch and smiled. Every summer she drug her house plants out as well as buy some annuals and herbs to put in pots. It was a chore to get them all watered, but she enjoyed the lush look it gave the space. It was feeling less like work and more like something worthwhile. One of her cats sat like a small loaf of bread, watching as she planted some of the starts from her spider plant into a new pot. It was hard for her to watch them go to waste. Plus, she liked giving the growing plants to others. Since Alice was a teacher, Lauren gave them to her kids at school to plant. So while it was sort of like an OCD thing for Lauren, she justified it by saying it was for educational purposes. Come to think of it, she could justify most all of her indulgent habits.

In the house, she heard Scout and Guinness wrestling. They were like gorillas in the house once they started playing. As Lauren finished primping her plants, their playing turned into the barking game. Lauren opened the back porch door, walked in and yelled, "Stop it, Freak Dogs!"

Just then she noticed that Franny Bottoms was about to knock on her front door with her cane. She froze when she heard Lauren yell. Lauren dashed to the door, apologized, and waved the older woman inside.

"Well, that was certainly some bellerin' you just did, Lauren." Franny hobbled in with a casserole dish and flowers.

It took a moment of absorbing the very loud housedress the woman was wearing before she realized how rude she was being, "Let me help you with that."

"Brought you some of my shredded chicken casserole–Ty's favorite," Franny grinned. With one arm free, she smothered the resisting Lauren in a hug. Lauren winced, not just from the unwanted affection but also from the unwanted food. The dogs sniffed the casserole with interest. However, once their noses processed it, their ears flattened and they backed away. Lauren looked at them with envy.

Please let me be gracious, Lauren thought as a half prayer. "Oh, Franny, you shouldn't have," she said as she set the dish down, "and I mean that."

"You don't get to town much, so I think you're not eating. I make sure you do," Franny said, proudly.

"With twenty dogs in the kennel, I don't have a lot of time. So, thanks." It hurt to say it. Franny seemed unaware that her food was inedible. But, Lauren appreciated her kindness. Even if it came with the price of having to entertain her for a while. Tyler always handled this before. Not for the first time, she missed having him as a buffer in social situations.

Franny pulled up a chair and flumped into it, propping her bright slippers on a chair, "Dogs don't make for much conversation."

"I know, but I'm really okay with that." Lauren found it hard to sit, knowing if she did she likely would lose a couple hours of her life she wouldn't get back. But it was already too late.

"Oh, I can only stay a minute," Franny said, but looked rather pointedly at the coffee maker on Lauren's counter.

Lauren took a deep breath, "How about I make some coffee?"

As she turned her back, Franny said, "By the way, Dear, I've found the nicest young man for you."

*

"How did I get talked into this?" Michael muttered under his breath. He'd been on the set since five in the morning, as the director wanted to use the first light of dawn for this scene. It figured the guy wanted to go the purist route and not rely on special effects like most did any more. If he wasn't so cold, Michael may have managed to appreciate the director's approach.

External shots like this were tricky, particularly since the scene had multiple parts and Michael needed to get as many takes right the first time or more early mornings were in his future.

The director approached him and put his arm over Michael's shoulders, "That was fine work, Mick. I really like the way you snickered at the homeless guy before you dropped him some money."

"It was a natural reaction, really. You didn't tell me he'd be holding a sign."

"That was his idea. He may not have a speaking role, but he sure was creative about making himself more visible."

The two men watched as the actor playing the homeless man walked by with a cardboard sign that read, "out of work super model."

"Are you ready for the chase scene? The thugs are down at that end and the dog will start chasing you about here."

"Dog?" Michael blinked at the director. He couldn't remember his agent telling him about a dog. Then again, his enthusiasm for getting the part may have drowned out any red flags in the script.

"Yeah, the police dog. Don't worry, Felicia is trained by the best."

Michael looked down the set and noticed the German shepherd dog watching the trainer as they walked over an area. Felicia? Such a tender name for a dog that looked like it could dismember him if she felt like it. Not for the first time this morning did Michael wonder if he should fire his agent. He looked at the director and put down his coffee, "Let's do this."

As the director went back to his chair, Michael busied himself at the snack table then headed to his mark. He looked down the set where he'd end his sprint. When he read that running would be a part of the story, he immediately doubled his training sessions. From past experience, he knew he didn't want to reshoot a scene that required repeated physical demands. He wasn't a spring chicken anymore, as his knees reminded him.

Michael glanced behind him at the two actors playing the thugs and the dog that was now under their care. The dog seemed to be doing a good job of getting into character as it already was barking at him. He was going to do everything in his power to make sure he got this on the first take. At least he wouldn't need to dig too deep for inspiration for showing fear.

As the set quieted and the cue sounded, Michael sprinted forward, his arms pumping fiercely by his side. He heard the two thugs yelling after him, and more importantly, the dog's nails digging into the pavement as its growl grew louder and louder.

The door frame in sight, Michael leapt onto the raised area and reached for the door handle. Exactly on time, the door banged open and a meaty arm shoved a pistol in his face. Michael raised his hands to surrender as the dog reached him.

Suddenly the growling stopped and the dog's tail wagged as it leapt onto Michael's chest, nuzzling his pocket.

The director screamed, "Cut!" He dashed to the door frame, "What was that?"

The dog trainer appeared, "Felicia, release!"

The dog instantly obeyed, but looked at Michael with hunger in her eyes.

The director turned on the trainer, "I thought you said she could stay ferocious."

"It's not her fault," Michael said. He reached into his pocket, retrieving a broken strip of bacon. "I was just trying to make friends."

The director, handler, and even the thugs made sounds of disgust as they walked away, getting fifteen minutes to rest before resetting the scene. The thug with the pistol dropped it at Michael's feet.

"I hate guns," Michael mumbled at the fallen prop as he stood up, limping toward the table that still held his coffee.

The director noticed, "You okay, Mickey?"

"Yeah, I'm fine."

"You sure? We can get a stunt actor."

"No! I do my own!" Michael snapped. He was known in the industry for his willingness to do it all. He wasn't about to give in to a silly charley horse in his left calf. With his back turned, Michael grimaced intensely. His expression didn't improve when he saw his agent, Tom, standing by the table.

"I can't afford you getting hurt, you know," Tom said, popping a piece of bacon in his mouth.

"Your concern for my welfare is truly touching."

"You can't afford it either."

The dog reappeared by Michael's side, wagging her tail and cocking her head to the side to add to her charm. "You're just using me too, aren't you?" He said before giving the dog what was left of the bacon.

"Hey! I was going to finish that." Tom snapped.

"She earned her money the honest way," Michael raised his eyebrow.

Tom clutched his chest with his hand, "Oh! That hurts! Agent jokes. I am in shock."

"How did I let you talk me into a sequel of 'Hunter Phillips, Private Eye' anyhow?" Michael sat in a chair.

"Why are you blaming me?" Tom rubbed his fingertips together, "Wasn't it a little thing called your house payment?"

"Just tell me there will be no 'Part Three.'"

"Ha! They'd have to get Blake Greer to play the part by then. Hunter Phillips doesn't age." Tom smirked, "Besides, if Jessica hadn't stepped in to fill for Kelly at the last minute, you wouldn't be working at all."

Michael shrugged, "Kelly said it was a 'strategic move' to back out. As if it made her look like she had something better. I don't care. Jessica's got more talent anyway. It's worked out perfectly."

"Talent. Image. Two different things. Although Kelly's vlog is so popular no wonder she backed out. Say what you will, the girl's strategy to stardom is working." Tom waved his hands aimlessly, "Speaking of which." He removed a tabloid from under his armpit and unfurled it for Michael to see the headline.

Michael looked at the picture of himself being straddled by a beautiful Latina. "Michael's New Love–Another Knife in Kelly's Back?" Michael tossed it back. "I wasn't getting a lap dance. That girl was paid to come onto me like that."

Tom looked at the picture, "Yeah, and I see how you were fighting her off tooth and nail. You must have been real scared."

"Not that it's a headline I'm after, but notice how they didn't report on the orphanage I visited while I was down there."

"Look, the public is still mad that you jilted America's Adorable Princess."

Michael rolled his eyes, "You mean because Kelly has dubbed herself that, people actually believe it?" Why did he even ask? He knew it was true. "Besides, the 'princess' spun it her way and won the public relations battle. She wants attention, even if it isn't based on any truth. If I'm as insufferable as she has claimed, why is she still living in my house?"

"Maybe you should fight back, Mickey," Tom stated.

"No way. It's not worth it."

"Not worth your reputation? The truth?"

Michael crossed his arms and gave Tom a hard look, "There is no truth in Hollywood." He paced a bit, "Besides, Kelly's just on her way up in this broken, pretend world. Why should I ruin her? My career can take it."

Tom raised his eyebrow, "You think so, do you? I just got off the phone with the producer of *Judge Hart*. You're out."

"What? It can't be that bad."

"It's bad, but not bottom of the barrel bad. You're not going to have to beg a role from Cecil Mercury any time soon."

The name of the disastrous director caused Michael to shudder. Any actor with even a microbe of integrity avoided him. "Cecil Mercury. He sounds like a British superhero."

*

An hour and counting, Lauren looked down at her phone to see the time. Would it be rude for her to text Alice and ask her to come save her? Would Franny even notice?

Meanwhile, Franny gabbed on, "So I asked, 'does a pound

cake really weigh a pound?' "

The squeal of car tires startled both of them. Lauren sprinted for the window, where she saw Franny's tiny Yorkie mix loping gleefully toward her house. The car owner yelled something out the window before driving on.

Lauren opened the door. "He's okay, Franny," she said as the old woman scooped the dog in her arms.

"Oh my little Goliath! My little man!" Franny snuggled the dog close. Guinness came over to sniff the small dog, wagging his giant tail.

"You really need to teach that dog some boundaries, Franny." Lauren said, hiding her frustration.

Franny tsked, "Oh no, I don't want to crush his spirit."

"If you don't, it's not his spirit that's going to be crushed." Lauren sighed. "Country roads are used more than they used to be. You should consider some training."

"I'll think about taking Goliath to class, Lauren, if you'll do something for me," Franny said, draining her coffee cup.

Lauren wondered what more she had to do besides be gracious with the casseroles. "What might that be, Franny?"

"Come back to Agnes Jane's Bible study."

"Oh, Agnes Jane," Lauren sighed. Now there was a woman who'd survived some trials. Alice told her to get out more and when she'd attended before Tyler's illness, it helped. And this was to keep Goliath safe, hopefully. "Deal."

Chapter Four–Understand Your Breed

Every session, each dog owner was asked to do a little research about the breed (or breeds) of the dog they brought to obedience class. Today's class featured the owner of the Bernese mountain dog.

"What I learned about my dog, Hercules, is that his breed was bred to be hearty and herd dairy cattle. They are good with children and are docile with strangers. They tend to bark a lot if they don't get enough exercise–and I know that is true. But they also are content to have a nice, quiet evening at home," the owner smiled at the group. "I also learned they are called Bernies. Isn't that cute?"

"And why did you choose this breed?" Lauren asked.

"Exactly for what the breed says–they are good with kids and friendly. I have a day care in my home, and I wanted a dog that would be friendly but could handle being outside if need be."

"Great, thanks. You and Hercules are a good match." Lauren looked around the room. "Sometimes we see a cute puppy and we pick it for looks alone. Only after that puppy begins to show its background do we sometimes realize that we've made a mistake." Lauren patted the square head of a large mixed terrier of questionable parentage.

"What's the best match, Lauren?" the terrier owner asked.

Lauren turned quickly and flashed a smile, "The best match is one based on true love. But, one must be smart about love. Just because someone or something is cute, doesn't mean it needs to be living in your home." Several class members snickered. Every session when Lauren brought out this point, it got some laughs and an occasional blush. People loved to talk about love.

The next day, Lauren noticed that the grass seemed to have grown two inches overnight. Fortunately, she didn't mind mowing as it gave her a chance to enjoy the flowering shrubs around the property. And think. For some reason, mowing allowed her brain to unwind. It was sort of relaxing, and it made her smile.

Of course optimism was short-lived for Lauren when she steered her mower past a missing board in the barn, the still broken downspout of the kennel, and some deep gashes in her yard from kennel clients who couldn't see the boundaries of the driveway beneath the snow. The work was never ending.

A rickety pickup truck pulled into the driveway. Lauren cut the engine of the mower and walked over to greet the older man who stepped from it. It wasn't unusual for people to drop by to ask about the kennel rather than calling first. Over the years, Lauren learned to look past this irritation.

"I'm Chet Carson, and I farm a few miles down the road

there," the man held out his hand and Lauren shook it, waiting to hear questions about the kennel.

"Yeah, so my son, Little Chet, just got divorced," Chet Carson said, stretching.

"I'm sorry to hear that, Mr. Carson," Lauren said. Great, she thought, the dog was likely caught in the middle. This could get tricky.

"You can call me Chet. It was Little Chet's fault. He was stepping out on his wife. Of course, t'weren't like she was home much. She liked the bingo, you know."

Lauren smiled politely, hoping the point of the conversation would come soon. She hated to think that the man might start telling her about the ex-wife's fondness for troll dolls and lucky blotters for her bingo habit. Some people loved unnecessary details.

"So, we wanted to know if you might come to supper to meet him. He's a nice guy."

"What?" It took Lauren some moments to realize that Chet Carson's visit had nothing to do with dogs whatsoever. "Oh, that's very kind but I'm afraid—"

"I should tell you he also lost his job as a plumber," the man continued. Lauren realized he wasn't listening to her.

"Business went down the drain, did it?" she quipped.

As she suspected, her little joke went unnoticed.

Chet Carson turned to admire the barn. "But he's got some good feeders this year, so things are good."

"Feeders? Like bird feeders?" Lauren frowned.

This caused the man to laugh and even slap his knee. "Heck, if Little Chet ever got hisself near a band saw, there's no tellin' what might happen besides a few lost finger digits."

As the man continued to laugh at the idea, Lauren started to feel like she needed an interpreter. Granted, she was raised in the city, but it was still the same state. But she had no idea what this man was talking about.

"Little Chet raises pigs as a hobby."

"Oh." Lauren didn't know what to say, but thought mentioning that stamp collecting seemed much cleaner might be a bad idea.

The man looked at her and raised an eyebrow, "That means he's gonna have a good pig harvest."

"That does sweeten the pot, but honestly, I'm not dating right now."

Again, Chet Carson seemed oblivious to her words and instead looked at the barn and whistled, "That sure is a nice barn. You could raise a lot of pigs in that barn."

Lauren covered her mouth with her hand. She didn't know if she was going to bust out laughing or break into hysterical tears. "Still going to have to say no."

Chet Carson shrugged his shoulders and got back into his truck and closed the door. He leaned out the window and pointed at the broken board, "You're going to need someone to help you keep up the property."

"Thanks for your concern, but I've got someone."

With one more covetous look toward the barn, Chet Carson left.

As Lauren returned to her mower, she swung one leg over the seat and plopped down with a sigh, "And that someone is not going to have an agenda."

After the feeling of annoyance left, Lauren snorted. Then, she couldn't stop laughing. She called Alice.

"I can't believe it," Alice half laughed, "He wanted you to have dinner with his unemployed, adulterous pig farmer son?"

Lauren sighed, "He looked at my barn like it was a dowry."

"That's just so…so…" Alice searched for the word.

"Gross?" Lauren offered.

"Primitive."

*

Michael sighed. The older he got, the worse the quality of the scripts he was offered. Why couldn't he be more like Clint Eastwood and have his pick of award worthy stories instead of this schlock?

Maybe after his premier coffee brewer finished its cycle and offered him the best cup of coffee of his day, he'd be more human. Until then, he sifted through a stack of scripts his agent brought him.

"Dysfunctional dad. Stupid dad. Dysfunctional…" Michael looked up at the clacking of heels. "Kelly?"

Kelly sauntered into the kitchen, a bandage across her nose from recent surgery. Behind her she toted a faux leopard skin suitcase. Michael looked past her to see another matching piece of luggage sitting by the door.

"What's up? You going on a trip or something?" Michael said, pouring the steaming hot Italian roast into his favorite mug. There were times when routine and familiarity were comforting.

Kelly pushed past him and took the mug from him, taking a sip, then crinkling her nose, "I don't know how you drink this stuff straight."

As she reached for the sugar, Michael swiped the mug back from her. Suddenly he was in no mood to share. In fact, his hackles were up. He looked her in the eye, waiting for an explanation.

She looked away in disgust, "Don't you ever sleep?"

"About as much as you eat," he replied quickly. "And what's up with your clothes? Those jeans are so tight they'd fit a preschooler."

Kelly crossed her arms and tossed her hair. She sure was getting good at putting on airs, a far cry from the woman she was when they first met.

"I'm taking that role. I don't care what you say."

Before he dropped his favorite mug, Michael managed to get it to the counter. "Vanna White's understudy? Are you out of your mind?"

"Millions will be watching me. It's what I've always wanted."

Michael got in her face, but only because she seemed about to slip away forever. "Rule number twenty: you have to choose whether you'll be an artist or celebrity—you can't be both."

Kelly pulled back, the look on her face pure contempt. "Rule number twenty-one: you're out of work—you got no street cred!"

"That's not a rule."

Kelly turned on her spiked heels and grabbed her baggage, "Good luck, Schleprock."

The door banged shut behind her. Michael picked his mug up again and took a sip. "Schleprock? Where did she hear that one?"

Buttons scratched at the door and yipped. The door quickly opened and Kelly scooped up her little dog. "I'm also auditioning for Flintstones: the musical."

Lynne E. Scott

Chapter Five–This May Hurt

When people dropped their dogs off for boarding, Lauren listened carefully to what the owners told her about their dog's behavior. Everyone thought their dog was more special than others. Of course, she knew this was true of parents and their children as well. When people told her their dog needed special handling, Lauren assured them she would do so, adding, "Just like I do for all the dogs."

Love was tricky that way.

"What method of training do you use in your obedience classes, Lauren?" the owner of a Jack Russell terrier asked her as he set down the dog's bag of food.

"I believe in using whatever method works for your dog that is effective and fair," Lauren answered, knowing the subject was an emotional one for some. "Every breed is different as is every dog within that breed. Finding the right communication method that works for both a dog and an owner is the method I use. I know some trainers don't believe in doing anything that may cause a dog any bit of pain. Certainly we are not trying to instill fear into a dog. But a moment of small pain can be a powerful learning tool."

The owner smiled, "I'm glad to hear that. Sounds like you know a strong-willed dog when you see one."

"Takes one to know one," Lauren laughed as the owner handed her the leash.

*

It was time. Actually, it was well past time. Tyler's clothes needed to go. Lauren wasn't very sentimental, so it wasn't like she opened the closet to look at them. In fact, the closet in the extra bedroom hadn't been opened in months. There were people in need of nice clothing. It was ridiculous for her to keep holding onto it. Yet she knew there was no way around the emotions that the task would evoke.

Twice before she'd tried to do this, but never got farther than removing one of his favorite shirts from a hanger. She wore it with constancy.

"Toughen up, Honey," she told herself. Finally in a mood that had more to do with being grumpy than calm and centered, Lauren went on a spree of packing up what was left of Tyler's clothes, shoes, and ball caps. She thought that if she did it quickly, maybe it would not hurt as much–sort of like tearing off a bandage.

Guinness followed her from room to room, taking a particular interest in the stuffed garbage bags once she filled one. As he sniffed, Lauren saw him wag his tail. She felt sure he still recognized Tyler's scent, and clearly it made the dog happy. Guinness always preferred Tyler's company and moped for months after his death.

"Hellloooooo!" Alice called from downstairs. Lauren heard the screen door close, so she dragged another filled garbage bag down the steps to greet Alice. Alice walked over to the small pile of filled bags that Lauren accumulated.

"What, so soon?" Alice teased. "Don't go doing anything rash."

Lauren tossed her a look, "Yep. Now you can quit nagging me."

"I'll quit nagging when I can get you to leave this house a little more often. Which reminds me, I'm heading to town. Need anything from the grocery store?"

"Actually, I've got a huge list of stuff I need to buy. It's too much for you to pick up so I will make myself go later. Plus, I need to get on these home repairs. That gutter spout hasn't fixed itself."

"What's brought this all on? Suddenly you're all about action."

Lauren shrugged and put the last of the garbage bags by the door, "It was just time. Besides, I can't have this place falling apart. It's bad for business, and that's bad for me."

Alice peered out the window, "I wish Jim were more handy. Unfortunately, he's hopeless at repairs."

"My list is fairly long, so it's too much for a friendly favor anyway."

Alice peered over her shoulder at the list, "Wow, that's going to cost you a fortune."

Lauren frowned at her, "Thanks, I sort of didn't need the reminder. I suppose if I was willing to barter going to dinner with the repairman I'd have a lower bill."

Alice raised an eyebrow, "Oh Honey. You know men want more than dinner." Lauren looked defeated so Alice added, "But I did have an idea for your financial pinch. Why don't you rent out Tyler's cabin? You know how his buddies always wanted to use it as a hunting cabin."

Lauren dropped the last sack she was holding and put her hands on her hips and gave Alice a glare, "Have you been breathing the toxic fumes of Franny's casserole?"

Alice shrugged, "What? It's not a bad idea. In fact, Jim always hears of faculty members who need temporary housing. I guess I should say this is his idea, not mine."

Lauren picked the sack back up and tied it shut, "Oh sure, the bank would probably like me to send in my mortgage payment now and then. But, Alice, a stranger? You know I hardly want people I know around me right now, let alone strangers."

"Come on, Lauren. It's not going to be any work for you. Jim and I will clean up the place and make all the arrangements. You just receive rent money, okay? And who knows, maybe he'll be cute."

"Puppies are cute," Lauren picked up one of Tyler's shirts and sniffed it. It was faded and worn out in the elbows, but she slipped it over her shoulders and hugged it close around her. "Puppies are also a lot of work."

Alice held up one of Tyler's old sweaters and looked over at Lauren, "Do you only remember the work? The hard stuff?"

Lauren leaned on the back of the sofa, her shoulders drooping with defeat, "Alice, please let's not make your next project my romantic life. I'm not interested. Besides, who wants to date a widow? Every guy thinks they won't be as good as the long lost husband."

"Fine, don't date. I'm not going to tell you what to do. And you can always un-decide later." Alice looked frustrated as she jammed the last of Tyler's clothes into a new bag.

Lauren felt a tiny bit guilty, but couldn't help laughing at one of Alice's made-up words, "Thanks. I'll let you know if I ever make an un-decision."

Alice looked up and laughed with her, "You know what I mean. Just because you don't have interest in it now doesn't mean you won't at some other point. A year isn't a magic number and then you're all healed up and ready for the next man in your life."

"If only it were that easy," Lauren said. "Besides, why do we need to always hurry onto the next thing? Tyler was a good husband. I can appreciate that for a long time. Apart from home repairs, I'm getting along pretty well on my own."

"It's not that a person needs to be married, I agree with you, Lauren," Alice said. "But you were a good wife. Some man might really enjoy being loved and loving you back. It can make life better is what I'm saying, not that it is what makes you a whole person."

Lauren sat down, "I know you're right, but I suppose the work and responsibility side of things is all I can remember for now."

Alice sat next to Lauren, "Did you ever find that letter of recommendation Tyler talked about?"

"You know he was always kidding about it. Even if he actually did it, what would I seriously do with it? Hand it out at a speed dating night?" Lauren leaned back and rubbed her temples.

Alice shrugged, "I don't know, it seems like an awfully romantic idea for a letter like that."

Lauren's eyes flew open and she leaned forward, "Tyler? Romantic? Oh please."

"He was romantic! I saw the little stick figure drawings he made for you. They were sweet."

Lauren smiled at the thought. "Okay, those were sweet. And I do miss caring for him. Everything else now seems so . . . ."

Alice helped Lauren search for the word, "Superficial?"

Lauren nodded half-heartedly, "Useless."

Alice took Lauren's hand, "Okay. Lauren, listen to me. At some point, you need to look at what you have in front of you instead of what you have lost. If you stay in the past, you will never move forward. You can't let this become your identity. Go out in public, let people give you sympathy and pat your hand and say 'you poor dear.' Get it over with. It's not like they are going to say it every time they see you. Life moves forward.

You're too young to be trapped at home, wrapped up in what was."

Lauren turned toward Alice, "Is that what I've been doing? I mean, I'm not a hermit or anything."

"No, you're not. You've done well. The first year is done and it's all about healing. The second year may even be more difficult because you do have to live your life."

"I know you're right, Alice. It's not that you aren't. I just don't have any notion as to what it means to live my life. I've spent a lot of time living while watching another person's body die. What you're talking about is almost too much for me to even wrap my mind around."

Alice stood and glanced at the pile of bagged clothing. "You want me to go with you to drop these off?"

Lauren shrugged, "I do. But I don't want to do that today. This is enough for now."

Alice shook her head, "Suit yourself."

Lauren shot her a sideways look, "Was that a pun?"

"Maybe," Alice quipped. "Jim and I are going to start on the cabin. What do you want us to do with Tyler's things?"

Lauren frowned, "There can't be too much in there. Just stuff it in a box and put it in the closet."

"You don't want to . . . ."

"No, I don't."

After Alice left, Lauren stared at the pile of garbage bags.

Then, she started to cry.

*

When Michael Quinlan began his career as a teenager, his agent doted on him. Of course, he was also making them both a lot of money. Over the years, the contact was less and less frequent, with Michael pressing his assistant to set up meetings rather than having to return his agent's calls. Certainly technology made a difference in how they communicated. However, Michael still liked to make a personal visit at least once a year for face to face conversations. He didn't know why he thought it mattered, he just sensed that it was important.

Tom kept his office modestly decorated. If he could afford more, he didn't spend it on lush furnishings. Michael appreciated that about him. Mostly, Tom was a practical, down to earth guy.

As Michael returned the small pile of scripts he rejected to Tom, he paced in front of his desk. "Why are they going straight to dvd with it? That's not going to look good for me."

Tom stacked the script pile neatly and shrugged, "The studio didn't know how to market it, so their advertising budget was cut to nothing."

Michael stopped and stared in disgust, "Honestly, Tom, there are people who have been convinced to spend millions of dollars on bottled water. What marketing genius couldn't sell an adventure film?"

"Alright, look, there's just a mentality out there that you're better for comedy."

"Can't I do something more authentic?"

Tom squinted, "You mean organic?"

Michael sunk into the nearest chair and sighed, "I don't really know what either of those terms mean. I just don't want to get trapped into always doing comedy. Sometimes I think it's, you know, cheap."

"Cheap?" Tom laughed, "Comedies make millions. Why else would they make every hit a sequel?"

Michael ran his hand through his hair and peered at the numerous pictures on Tom's desk. He and his wife, his kids, the whole family and even a dog were proudly displayed.

Tom tossed a script to Michael. He didn't bother to turn the page after reading, the title, "My Science Teacher is from Venus." Michael shot to his feet, "I'm being relegated to after school specials?"

"Lots of actors your age are getting into television." Tom said, "It's much more respectable than before."

"My age?"

"Alright, there are other possibilities. And just to keep you in the loop, there haven't been after school specials for several decades now. But, reality shows are still very popular and I know one looking for a host."

"Never," Michael felt like he'd been punched in the stomach. Reality Show Host. When he was just getting started, he and his friends mocked them. His friends, who he no longer heard from, probably embraced them.

Tom shook his head, "I got nothing. But you better get that chip off your shoulder. No one wants that attitude. Why don't you work on getting your spark back?"

Michael tossed the script back and headed for the door, "Worst pep talk ever, Tom."

"You wanted authentic, I gave it to you."

"It's just feeling like I'm being used for my name and not my talent. Studios, women. Who am I supposed to trust? I'm so tired of this system."

Just then Tom's assistant came in and brought them both coffees. Michael noticed how she didn't even look in his direction. Couldn't he even turn a pretty girl's head anymore?

Tom leaned back and took a sip. He looked Michael up and down, then asked, "Mick, have you ever heard of the 'Cape Theory?'"

Michael rolled his eyes, "Oh, here we go. Where's this from?"

"It's carefully researched," Tom replied, playfulness creeping into his voice. "You know, Elvis had all these people around him and you know they were saying to him early on, 'you look good, Buddy!' Elvis gets a bit more famous, does some stupid movies, and his friends say, 'you look good, Buddy!' Then Elvis wears those rhinestone outfits and the friends say, 'you look good, Buddy!'"

Michael sighed, "Then Elvis wore the capes."

"Yep, and still his friends tell him, 'you look good, Buddy!'"

But he doesn't, he looks ridiculous. No one would tell him the truth about the state of his career and that he looked like an idiot. As long as tickets were being sold, nothing else mattered to the so called friends."

"What are you telling me, Tommy? Am I heading for a code red rhinestone alert?"

Tom smirked, "Not quite, Mick. You're more like at that 'sideburns don't become you' level. But you really need to get your head together."

Michael bristled, "I hate that phrase."

"Then just take a break. Here, take this," Tom gave him a business card. "That's my brother. He's a theater professor in some small town."

"'Some' small town? That doesn't sound promising." Michael tucked the card into his pocket, "Good bye, civilization. Hello, Bubba."

"No one will bother you there is what I'm saying."

Michael looked at Tom sideways, "Is that a comment on my career? I'm unrecognizable?"

Tom stood and leaned over his desk and looked Michael straight in the eye, "They are doing summer stock, Mick. Go back to your roots. Go see the reason you got into this business in the first place."

Michael nodded and stood, knowing it was the truth but not wanting to think too hard about it yet. He man-hugged Tom, "You're a good friend, Tom."

Tom clapped Michael on the back, "Look, Mick, I'm not your friend. I'm your agent."

After Michael left, a wave of loneliness hit him. Tom was the closest thing to a friend that he had right now. And that person wouldn't claim his friendship back. Certainly leaving couldn't make matters any worse.

Chapter Six–Sit!

The class assembled in the same order as they always did. Lauren smiled to herself. After five years of holding obedience classes, she still enjoyed watching how people gravitated into familiar patterns. She couldn't blame them–the fewer decisions she made in a day, the better.

"Who did their homework?" Lauren asked as she counted raised hands. "Six out of eight owners. That's pretty good. Now don't lie to me, because I'm going to find out when I work with your dog." The Lab owner's hand went down. Lauren grinned, "Five out of eight, that's still more than half."

"Can I have Jazzy's leash?" Lauren extended her hand to the Lab owner.

"This is Tucker, not Jazzy," he said indignantly.

"Sorry, Jazzy was last session," Lauren apologized, not wanting to admit that sometimes dogs looked alike and time went too fast for her to keep them straight.

The Lab owner said, "I did most of the homework, but I don't think we actually did twenty sits a day. It was closer to ten. I mean, that's still a lot." A couple of class members clapped their hands, which caused great excitement in some of the dogs.

"Does a dog really need to sit twenty times a day? I mean, it seemed like overkill," the owner of the Bernese mountain dog quipped.

"The purpose of this exercise is to get your dog to listen to you. That you've taught your dog to sit reliably is a happy result. Sit is an easy command for a dog to learn. When you repeat the exercise over and over, it teaches your dog to pay attention to you. The more your dog pays attention to you, the more you will be able to teach your dog. That's why we start here."

Lauren then instructed the group to walk in a large circle with their dog on the left side. She called out, "Sit" every so often and the owners would quickly stop. Most dogs clearly understood the expectation. A few did not, and their owners glanced at Lauren with guilty smiles as they coaxed their dogs' bottoms to touch the floor.

After a few more drills and showing how to teach a dog the "down" command, Lauren said, "This week's homework is about the down position but still continuing to reinforce 'sit.' However, think about when you are asking your dog to sit. This is the way your dog says 'please.' If your dog wants to go outside, he has to sit. If he wants a treat, he has to sit for it. In other words, your dog has to earn your attention. Remember, this is all about changing the way you two interact. When you trust each other, obedience follows naturally, not with strong-arming your own way."

*

"Your little spurt of productivity sure ended quickly," Alice said as she helped load the bags into the back of her small car.

"Sorry, it took a bit more out of me than I anticipated. Then my enthusiasm left me," Lauren answered. "But, I'm finally done and I want it out. It seemed cruel to have Guinness sniff the bags and wag his tail. It's sort of creepy, too, that dogs can still smell a scent for so long."

Alice added, "You'll be so glad to cross this off your list. I know how you are with lists."

Lauren grinned. She did love lists. Of course with the stress and amount of things to do every day, she relied on lists to get her through. Now that her physical load was lifted with Tyler's passing, she found her brain wasn't willing to work very well, so lists were again a necessity. There was a pleasant sense of accomplishment as well. Sometimes she'd do something that wasn't on her list. Then she'd write it on her list and cross it off, just for the sense of satisfaction.

"Does that seem weird to you?" she asked Alice.

Alice shook her head, "I hope not because I do the same thing."

Lauren smiled and looked ahead as Alice pulled out of her driveway. "This is why we're friends. Thanks for driving."

"I figured you'd be worn out. It's no problem," Alice hit the accelerator as soon as she turned onto the road.

Lauren frowned, "Why did Jim think getting you a sports car was a good idea?" She forgot that Alice drove like a Nascar driver, but was reminded as they made their way to the highway.

Alice tended to speed up when she was talking about something that excited her. While describing how promising her pumpkin patch was this year due to all the rain in the spring, she sailed close to seventy miles per hour until Lauren shrieked at her to slow down.

Finally they arrived at the charity, and Lauren removed her nails from where they'd dug into the upholstery. A few times she thought of jumping from the vehicle.

Lauren felt a little wobbly from her nerves after she got out. At least fearing for her life distracted her from becoming emotional over Tyler's clothing. It was just so personal, his clothing. So many memories were tied up with silly things like his favorite shirts.

"Let's find out where they want these before we carry all these bags in," Alice said.

Lauren sighed, "I hope I don't have to fill out a bunch of paperwork."

Alice scanned Lauren's raggedy jeans and Tyler's shirt over her T-shirt. "Where did you get that bruise?" she asked after seeing a new one on her arm.

Lauren paused and turned her arm over to look at it, "This one is from pinching my arm in a gate after a German shepherd came bolting out of the door."

"You're right, you do have excitement in your life." Alice said, "Maybe we could update your wardrobe while we're here."

Lauren turned to Alice, "That would make two of us, Pumpkin Girl." With a deep breath, she opened the door and walked up to the clerk.

"I need some help," Lauren said, noticing Alice was side tracked by a gingham shirt.

The clerk gave Lauren the once over carefully. She smiled indulgently, "That's why we're here, Dear. Follow me."

Lauren followed her through a doorway.

Alice looked up from a shirt in time to see Lauren and the clerk disappear. When the door shut, she saw the sign on it—"Counseling."

"Uh-oh," Alice froze.

Sure enough, Lauren bolted out the door, her face red. "I'm doing just fine!"

The clerk tried to catch Lauren, but she was out the front door. She turned to Alice and clucked her tongue, "Typical addict—in denial."

Alice crossed her arms, "She's not an addict. She's a widow dropping off her husband's clothes."

The clerk frowned, "Oh, I guess that explains her strung out look. What about that bruise?"

"She works with dogs."

"Oh," the clerk looked ruefully, "I'm sorry. She just looks battered."

Alice sighed, "I guess you could say in some ways she is."

Lauren stayed in the car while Alice and another volunteer

unloaded the bags. The counselor tapped on the rolled up window, in an attempt to apologize. Lauren finally nodded but quickly returned to stare into space.

Back on the road, Alice said, "Of all the things that could have gone wrong, I just didn't see that one coming."

Lauren stared out the window, "Story of my life." Her fingers again dug into the fabric on the seat, wondering if the other small tears were from past passengers.

"Jim told me your tenant is in the cabin. Don't be alarmed if you see activity back there."

Lauren half-smiled to her friend, "Can we call them 'your tenant?' I don't want anything to do with that situation. I'm grateful you've arranged it, but I just don't want any more messes right now."

"Give yourself a break. You really are doing just fine," Alice reached over and gave Lauren's arm a light squeeze.

"Ouch! That's my bruise," Lauren rubbed the spot but laughed. "Oh, Alice. I'm not as fine as you may think. This morning at breakfast I was so out of it that when I brought my spoon up from my bowl of cereal, I realized that it was dog kibble. I looked over at Scout and he was eating my granola. Yeah, I'm doing just fine indeed!"

Alice laughed and shook her head. "But we all have bad days."

"You don't understand. My brain is just not operating like it should." Lauren looked over at Alice. "And did you see the article in today's paper about some study showing that surviving spouses face shorter life spans? How'd you like to wake up to that headline?"

*

After further discussions with Tom, Michael decided that leaving the safety zone of southern California was a good idea. It wasn't his first choice, but even he could see he was stuck in a rut. He realized that while he spent most of his career wanting anonymity from the paparazzi and privacy from fans, when he was no longer the hot topic, he missed it all over again. While he didn't miss Kelly, he missed the idea of Kelly. More stuff to mess with his head, which complicated his already frustrated emotions.

He thought about driving across country, but that seemed more demanding than what he reasonably could handle. After all he wasn't altogether hearty with door-to-door service to airports where he was able to take the VIP route to the plane. Rubbing elbows with "common folk," as Tom said, was not something he'd done for a while. And small town people. Why didn't they move somewhere exciting? He hoped he could survive the illiterates. Certainly if they had any real skills, they would have moved away.

Fortunately, one of his brothers still lived in a big city in the Midwest. Even though Michael didn't visit him often, he kept a car there so he'd have his own set of wheels. He picked up his car, which was ordinary by Hollywood standards, but still a step above the sensibilities and practicalities of a good Midwesterner. However, Michael noticed more and more "status cars" in the bigger cities. Whether the owners could afford them or not, there were more on the road. Michael was just glad that he was fitting in when he set out for a town that likely wouldn't be on the map without the presence of the local college.

As he drove farther from his brother's, the scenery quickly changed to cornfields. He'd been told that relying on GPS to guide him would only get him lost. The roads were marked by numbers or letters, if they were marked at all. There were no landmarks to speak of to help. Fortunately, the directions Jim, Tom's brother, sent him were accurate.

He sensed he was getting closer as even fast food restaurants were rare. He glanced at his map and he looked to be only five miles from his destination. On a narrow country road, he noticed the drivers of the pickup trucks coming toward him often raised their hand from the steering wheel in a half-wave. How could they recognize him out here? Did someone alert the local media? Had he been followed or spotted so there were Twitter reports as to his whereabouts? He called Tom.

"For Pete's sake, Mick. They are farmers. They wave at everyone."

Michael felt mildly embarrassed, thinking again he was the center of the universe. Would he ever break that mindset? He looked across the vast farmland. "If this background had a sound track, it would be *Dueling Banjos*."

"And you were worried about what you'd do with all your free time," Tom mocked.

"Seriously. What am I going to do all day?" Michael packed his basic electrical gadgets, but still.

"Jim would probably love some help. Why don't you go see

him?"

"Maybe. What am I going to do all night?" This thought was even worse to him.

Tom sighed impatiently, "There's this thing that the rest of mankind does. Sleep. It's what you do when you have a normal routine."

"You are a lousy friend."

"Have I ever coddled you or told you less than the truth?"

"No, you're right. I'm glad you're honest. Usually." Michael glanced at the paper and realized he was almost to the cabin. He felt strangely nervous.

"Jim said the cabin is unlocked and to just settle right in. You don't have to see anyone if you don't want to. He left a list of numbers and places to get food. Now remember when you get there, there's no valet service. You'll have to carry your own baggage."

When Michael hung up with Tom, he considered that dealing with his own baggage was exactly why he was at this remote place. He steered carefully along the long gravel driveway until he spotted the cabin. Once, a director invited the cast of a movie to her Aspen "cabin," which was about thirty thousand square feet. This one looked about seven hundred. Instead of looking at mountain tops, he was surrounded on three sides by rows of corn. It was like a green fence. This was different privacy than what he expected.

As he popped the trunk to grab his bags, he used his best Elvis voice to mutter to himself, "I look good, Buddy."

The inside of the cabin was a welcome sight. Rugged in a good way, there wasn't paneling but the actual logs. It even smelled good. Taking a tour of the small kitchen and living area along with one bedroom and bathroom took about five minutes. He set his bags down and wondered, "Now what?"

Off the kitchen was a door which opened out on a large back porch. On it were some simple chairs and table. The view was still cornfields, but a few trees and shrubs rounded out the landscape nicely.

Michael sat, taking in the scenery. The one thing he noticed the most was the quiet. There was no sound but the husks of corn blowing in the light breeze and the occasional bug zipping past.

Among the notes Jim left on a table in the cabin, there was the thinnest phone book Michael had ever seen. He picked it up and thumbed through it. It didn't take long, and the one thing he noticed was the absence of any plastic surgeons in the listings. Kelly would hate this place.

Next, he found the local newspaper. Michael noticed it came out once a week. "Well, that gives me something to look forward to anyway." He read the headline, "College Student Survives Fatal Crash." Michael read it twice. Yes, nonsensical headlines like this would definitely have him buying the paper.

A cacophony of barking dogs broke the silence, sending Michael to his feet. The sound echoed around him, and he couldn't find where it began or ended. He darted inside the cabin and looked outside. He didn't want to get attacked by a pack of wild dogs on the first day.

He opened the door slightly, noticing the sound didn't seem to be getting closer or farther. After a moment, he returned outside. With a shrug of his shoulders, and no longer concerned about an attack, Michael opened the paper to read the weekly report by the local police. Now there was some good reading.

Chapter Seven–Down!

"It's a useful command, but a tough one for the dog to obey." Lauren took Guinness to the center of the room where he sat after Lauren's prompting. "Begin with a 'sit' then tell your dog 'down,' " she said, at the same time moving her straight arm toward the ground. Guinness stretched out his front legs and laid down, his eyes on her.

After allowing the class to try the method a few times, she walked around the room to demonstrate different techniques suitable for each of their dogs.

"Why is it so hard for them to learn?" Wendy asked, still fighting Sparky, who only partially would move toward a 'down.' No wonder they were back for a second time through training. Wendy lacked the nerve to be strict with her dog.

Lauren stepped back to answer the question for the whole room. " 'Down' requires the dog to give up more control. If they are sitting and want to quickly get away from danger or chase something interesting, it's much easier. A dog may be uncomfortable when you ask them to do this because they are more vulnerable. But the more you ask of them, the more they will obey."

After giving herself a pep talk, Lauren bravely went to Kettlesville for food. However, she just wasn't ready for the grocery store. So she went to the carry out instead. Maybe it wasn't the healthiest of choices, but their breakfast biscuits were surprisingly good, even if their machine cappuccino left much to be desired. Happily, the jaunt was uneventful.

Just as she turned onto her road, she noticed something running alongside the road near her home. It moved too fast to be one of her cats, and its gait was peculiar enough not to be that of a dog. She approached it slowly, the sound of the truck engine inciting the creature to move faster. Finally, Lauren pulled even with the scared creature. A pig. A small, pink pig. Trotting down the road for all its worth.

Fortunately, it was headed for her house. Wanting to pass it so she could get out of her truck, Lauren honked the horn. Not knowing how a pig might respond to this, she was happy to see it move to the right. What an obedient little pig. If only all drivers were so cooperative.

She passed the pig and pulled into her driveway. Jumping from her truck, she ran to the road, just as the pig raced by. Lauren chased after it.

They passed the long driveway that led to Tyler's cabin, and Lauren wondered just how much endurance this pig had. Mostly she wondered how much she had. Just as the pig approached Franny Bottoms' home, a car came racing from the other direction.

"Pig! Pig!" Lauren yelled and waved her arms in the air. The car swerved around them, but the pig squealed, reversed direction, and zipped by Lauren.

Lauren stopped, panted, and contemplated why she cared about this stupid animal. But, she turned and chased after the pig, racing past the long driveway again. "Pig! Stop pig! I'm going to throw up!"

*

Michael's sudoku book lost all interest to him. Sitting on the back porch, he'd just witnessed a woman running back and forth on the road after a pig. Was this what people did around here for fun?

*

The pig disappeared into the hedgerow by her home. Lauren slowed to a walk and approached it to search for the small pig.

The hedges were too thick for her to see well, but she thought she heard the rustling of something that must be the piglet. Not really having a plan or any knowledge of pig rustling, she went with the only option she could think of–Scout. She dashed into the house, calling him to her. Being the mostly obedient dog that he was, Scout appeared instantly, seeming to know he was needed.

"Let's go," she said as he darted out the door and down the front steps of her porch. "You're just not going to believe this one." He glanced at her before catching the scent of something new. Nose to the ground, he followed the path the pig ran earlier.

Scout's hackles raised as he darted into the bushes, growling.

It dawned on Lauren that her plan was not a very good one. What was a dog going to do? Would it kill the piglet? Would the piglet kill the dog? Completely out of her element, Lauren pulled out her cell phone and quickly called her friend Tish.

"There's a pig in my bushes!" Lauren yelled.

"Is that code?" Tish asked with a laugh.

"No, there is really a little pig hiding in the bushes by my house."

"How would I know what to do?" Tish wondered.

"I thought pharmacists knew everything." Strike two.

"I could help you with swine flu, Lauren, but not swine. Did you call Alice? She has chickens. Call her."

"Does she know about pigs?"

"I don't know, but both live in a barn." Tish said, "Besides, I'm in Vegas for a conference."

Lauren followed Tish's orders. She called Alice, who, after hearing the strange situation, said, "I'll be right over."

"Bring a net." Lauren said, not knowing why.

Scout dove into the bushes, then quickly backed out with a whimper as the pig lunged with an indignant grunt. Lauren realized pigs were not likely to be herded with any precision, so she called the dog to her, putting Scout back into the house. She could see his two little ears pricked at attention at the front door as she returned to the hedge row. Guinness joined Scout, both staring out the window, calmly watching the drama.

Alice's sports car revved, heralding its arrival before Lauren saw it. What a comfort that her own pickup was old and rickety. In the country, the older and louder the pickup, the more noble the owner. Lauren felt very noble.

The sound caused the piglet to bolt from its hiding place. It shot right into another group of shrubs around Lauren's home. Alice got out and handed Lauren a net. "Is this a pig getting net?" she asked.

"It's a trout fishing net," Alice responded as she pulled plastic fencing from the back of her car.

"You trout fish?" Lauren's day seemed surreal.

"Jim does, now take this end," Alice handed her the end of the plastic fencing and the two women constructed an area in which they could corner the piglet with the fencing. Now all they had to do was drive it into the area.

"Pig-pig-pig-pig!" Alice yelled.

Lauren picked up the net and looked at her. "Is that a thing?"

Alice shrugged.

Lauren frowned, "It's not like kitty-kitty-kitty, the international language of cats."

"Pig-pig-pig-pig!"

"I can't believe this," Lauren said, assessing the situation. "How much education do we have among us and we can't catch a pig?"

Alice's brow furrowed, "It's 'between' us not 'among' us. There's just two of us. If there were more than two, then it would be 'among.'"

Lauren shook her head, "Uh-huh. Thanks, Grammar Nazi."

Just then Alice rushed the shrubs at a mad dash and random squawks, resulting in a squeal by the pig as it sprinted from its hiding place, directly into the fenced in area.

"Close the gate! Close the gate!" Alice yelled.

Lauren looked at Alice, "Gate? We don't have a gate."

"Make a gate! Make a gate!" Alice yelled.

Alice looked around and grabbed the trash can on Lauren's back porch. She laid it on its side to block the pig from dashing out of the small area. Just like that, the pig scampered into the garbage can. With a whoop of victory, Alice righted the garbage can, the pig secured at the bottom.

Lauren peered into the can cautiously. "Will it jump out?" she asked.

Alice drew herself up straight, "Nope."

"I can't believe it. We caught a pig," Lauren said.

"Excuse me, but I believe it was I who caught the pig," Alice said.

"You're absolutely right, Alice." Lauren patted her arm, "And the reward for your cunning bravery is you get to keep it."

Alice shook her head, "What am I going to do with a piglet? Lauren, Tyler said if a creature stepped foot on your property—"

Lauren looked alarmed, "I can give him away to friends."

Alice stared down at the pig. "He is kind of cute."

"How do you know it's a he?" Lauren challenged.

"You said he was running down the road. I figured it has to be male if he's trying to get away."

Lauren shook her head and smiled, "How did my life get so weird?"

*

The quaintness of the weekly newspaper could only entertain him for so long, and not just because it was less than ten pages of content. There weren't many places left in the country where cell phone service was unreliable, but Michael landed in one. Since his phone apps for music proved spotty, he discovered a local station on the small radio in the cabin. The word "campy" came to mind. It was truly a mix of music, and the local announcers enjoyed creating their lead-ins from one song to another by using lyrics from the songs.

"And that was 'Laughter in the Rain.' Let's hope you are walking hand in hand with the one YOU love. More music on the way in sixty seconds."

Of course campy could be wearing, so that soon lost his interest. After a couple of days of politely ignoring the box of items stuffed in the hallway closet, Michael pushed his way in to get a closer look. There were items like yearbooks, trophies, and an old guitar in the far corner piqued his curiosity. He'd read enough scripts to know that little touches like this indicated a bigger story. However, he didn't want to intrude too much, even though he was tempted.

Michael wasn't one to keep a personal assistant after a few failed experiments. Eventually he managed to talk Tom into piecing out the minimum responsibilities to his staff for a small additional fee. However, it resulted in Michael having limited personal contact information for some of his buddies. He had few close friends. In fact, it seemed like he had none that were truly trustworthy.

After resisting for hours, he flipped open his laptop and found a signal. He searched around on YouTube and found the most recent viral hit, titled "Puzzling Pass." Michael clicked on it.

Kelly and Vanna stood on either side of the giant letter puzzle and clapped politely while the contestant spun the wheel. After calling out a letter, the two women pressed lights to make letters appear and began to pass each other to trade sides. The video then shows Kelly's foot turn ever so slightly, and Vanna tripped and fell flat on her face. Kelly turned to express surprise. Michael knew that look. Kelly was definitely feigning her shock as she reached her hand down to help Vanna back to her feet.

He read a few of the comments below the video. Normally he ignored them, but he didn't have hours to kill either. While it was nice to see how forgiving people could be, the vehemence with which some people labeled the two women was horrifying, even to him. It was as if every civility had died. What was the most heartbreaking was the number of people who dismissed Vanna as being too old. Kelly's youthfulness was better. Of course it was put more bluntly with ruder language and more misspelled words than he could ever imagine. He wondered if Kelly or her friends made some of those comments. He wouldn't put it past her to enlist her minions.

His stomach clenched in a knot and he closed his laptop. Maybe the lack of reliable internet was a good thing. He couldn't believe how quickly Kelly gained fame. And now he was in the middle of nowhere.

"Yoohoo!" a knock on the cabin front door jarred Michael from his disturbing thoughts. He didn't know who it was, but he was thankful.

Michael opened the door to an older woman wearing some sort of colorful muumuu. The woman pressed a still warm casserole dish in his hands as she squeezed past him and into the room, which suddenly seemed much smaller. It took him a moment to notice a small dog swirling around her feet.

"I'm Franny Bottoms. Nice to meet you, New Neighbor." She stood staring at him, and finally he realized that he needed to say something. Should he use an alias? She didn't seem to recognize him, but he thought that was probably a good thing.

"Hi, I'm Mickey."

Franny assessed him with narrowed eyes. She pointed a chubby finger at him, "Eeconomonics!"

"What?" He wondered if she was putting a hex on him. Tom didn't mention the area being rife with witches, but then again, they weren't so uncommon in LA either. He did mention Amish. Maybe this was their secret language he'd read about.

"You're an eeconomononics professor, ain't ya? I can always

tell!" Franny smiled proudly.

Michael winced. Did he look like a business guy? Before he could be too concerned, Franny grabbed the casserole out of his hands and waddled toward the kitchen. "This here is my famous shredded chicken casserole. It's the talk of the county, it is!"

"Why would anyone shred a chicken?" Michael mumbled.

"What's that?"

"I said, it sets my heart a tickin'." He grinned, hoping his acting proved convincing.

Franny took the few steps back into the living room and looked around disapprovingly. Her dog rooted through the duffle bag Michael left on the floor. "Goliath! Get!" The dog immediately ran to her and accepted a treat from her.

"Your wife okay with this place? Awful small."

Michael appreciated the subtle ways people coaxed information from him. However, he figured that in Franny's world, men his age were normally married, so it wasn't too great of a leap.

"No wife, just me."

Franny swung around, her eyebrows high on her forehead, "Really? Perhaps you'd like to meet our Dog Lady?"

Michael inwardly cringed. He wondered if she was referring to a carnival side show act, "She must be quite a looker."

"What's that?" Franny asked.

"I can't believe no one else has took her."

Franny waved a hand at him, "Oh, Lauren is just difficult. But, I'm sure she's a fine landlord for ya." She opened the door and called her dog, "Nice to meet you, Ricky!"

As he watched her walk down the driveway, Michael noticed a peculiar odor. Had he left the oven on? Was someone using turpentine? Michael sniffed around, wondering if he should call either the fire department or poison control. However, he soon discovered there was no need to alert the authorities, it was only Franny's famous casserole.

Lynne E. Scott

Chapter Eight–Fear Biters

Lauren spent the first part of each class allowing the owners some time to discuss problems they experienced with their dogs which may or may not be related to their weekly "homework."

Melanie's dog, Callie, cowered behind her legs for the first two weeks of class. Though most border collies were intelligent and strong-willed, this little mix was fearful. Not knowing whether this fear was from a history of abuse or lack of socialization, Lauren proceeded with caution whenever she interacted with the dog. While Callie made some progress, there was a long way for her to go to be a trustworthy dog.

"Last weekend, my sister was over. She tried to pet Callie, but Callie snapped at her." Melanie's voice shook, "I just don't know what to do. I don't want to give her up."

"What you are describing is called 'fear biting' and it's not uncommon. Having her in class for training is a great idea. Was she a rescue dog?" Lauren asked.

"I got her from the pound. I felt bad for her because she hid in the back of the cage," Melanie said. "She's okay with me, but every now and then I'm afraid of her too. It's been six months that I've had her. Shouldn't she trust me by now?"

"You don't know what's happened in her past, but minimally, she's got trust issues. They may run deep." Lauren walked alongside Melanie as the group began to walk in a large circle. She gently took the leash from Melanie and took her place as they walked. Callie hunched low to the floor when she realized her owner was gone, but Lauren walked faster, even passing other dogs and owners. Callie had no choice but to keep walking. Lauren didn't look at her, just praised Callie for how well she heeled by her side.

"Training builds confidence for the dog. Here she's getting both mental and physical challenges, which mean she's moving and thinking. She doesn't have time to think about what's made her afraid. Instead, she's building a bond with the owner. When she trusts her owner, she can learn to trust others."

*

By the fifth night of Michael's stay in the country, he was both bored and curious. Every so often, the sound of dogs barking pierced the air. It went on for a long time, then it stopped. Finally, he decided to investigate.

Stepping off his back porch, he listened as the dogs started their evening cacophony. He looked at the time–nine thirty. Always it began at nine thirty. There was a small path that cut through the cornfield where water flowed through a small ditch. He followed it in the fading daylight until the sound of barking grew louder. He noticed another path and followed it cautiously.

He emerged from the cover of the cornfield and the narrow

path into another yard. He was pretty sure this was considered trespassing. However, he could use a little excitement in his life, so he crept behind a tree and looked into an outbuilding from which light poured. Here it was—he discovered ground zero of the barking. He saw a figure moving back and forth inside, so he approached for a better view.

Before he took another step, a low growl came from behind him. He wasn't on a movie set any more and there was no trainer to call off whatever beast spotted him. He assessed his options before slowly turning his head. At the same time, the large black form charged him. Michael bolted for the barn that was beside the outbuilding, which fortunately had an old wooden ladder leading up to who knew where. He scaled it in seconds, relieved to find a neat hayloft. Michael stepped off the top of the ladder to see the black dog barking furiously.

The dog's paws were on a rung of the ladder and it lunged as if it would climb it. Michael flung the top of the ladder away, and the dog backed off as it fell. It only took Michael another second to realize what a stupid move he made.

"Great, thanks, Cujo!" He hissed at the still barking dog.

The faint light from the building went out, preventing Michael from seeing the dog. The door to the outbuilding creaked open. The barn light allowed him to see a figure emerge. Being the brave soul that he was, he hid behind a hay bale.

The black dog continued to bark, and was joined by the growling and barking of another dog

"Guinness, Scout, knock it off. You find another raccoon?"

the woman's voice reprimanded, but to no avail. She turned off the barn light, the darkness finally quieting the dog.

Realizing things weren't looking good for him, Michael hastily called, "Hellloooo?"

The woman shrieked as the dog's barking intensified. Michael heard a rummaging sound, then the tell-tale sound of a gun being cocked.

"I'm really sorry, but I'm living next door."

The faint light gradually glowed bright again. Michael peered from behind the hay bale and noticed a young woman peeking from behind a barn post.

"Who are you? I've got a gun!"

She didn't seem hysterical, which in Michael's book meant she was more dangerous. He cursed his stupidity, but decided to try his powers of persuasion one more time, "I'm your neighbor, I swear."

"I know my neighbors. You're not one of them."

"Could you put the gun down?" Michael could see the barrel of the gun, and it was pointed right at him. He couldn't remember the last time he felt this scared in real life. A momentary thought flickered through his brain that the next time he got a role in which he needed to act terrified, he would know exactly what to do.

"I'll lower my gun when you tell me who you are and what you're doing on my property at night, you freak."

"This is so embarrassing," Michael said.

"Be embarrassed or be shot. Your choice," the woman said, still calm and collected.

The light from the lamp illuminated the woman. Maybe it was her feisty demeanor, but he noticed she was on the cute side, despite the well-worn jeans. "Easy, Killer. I'm renting that cabin next door."

The woman took a step forward and squinted up, "That's my cabin. What are you doing snooping?"

Just then the smaller dog circled the woman's legs, tripping her backwards, "Oh shoot!" The gun fired as she fell. Michael leapt back behind the hay bale.

"Nice job, Annie Oakley," Michael said as he picked straw from his hair.

"And you are Peeping Tom!"

Michael winced, "You heard that, huh?" He stepped out from behind the hay.

Lauren squinted, "Mick Quinlan?"

"Hey, at least you know I'm good for the rent." Michael shrugged, hoping he looked contrite yet charming. "You can call me Mickey."

The woman looked doubtful, "I can call the police."

"No!" Michael mentally shuddered, anticipating what tabloids would do with a story this bizarre. While he wasn't at the top of his career right now, anything weird always made news. And this situation qualified. "Look, I can't afford to have this be headline news. I'll give you money–anything–but you need to keep this quiet!"

The woman lowered her gun, "I don't need anything."

Finally the conversation he had with Franny Bottoms gelled, "So, you're the Dog Lady?"

"I prefer to go by Lauren."

"You should go by Pit Bull Lady."

Lauren crossed her arms and leaned against the pole, "Wow, you charm women with lines like those? They must just fall at your feet."

This irked Michael, "Generally I don't have an issue with women pointing a gun at my heart."

Lauren snorted, "What heart?" She glanced at her dogs, "Congratulations, Guinness, you've treed your first movie star."

The dog wagged his tail at her.

"Yes, I see they are very proud, now could you put the ladder back up for me?"

Lauren stood, "I could." But she didn't. Instead, she flipped off the light and called the dogs after her, and they obediently complied.

As Michael heard the jingle of the dog tags fade in the dark, he considered his limited options. Jumping would likely result in minimally ruined ankles. He wasn't exactly in a position to have someone nurse him back to health. Considering the one woman he met seemed to have limited mobility and was a bad cook and the other toted a gun and seemed hostile, he opted to stay put.

Surely in the light of day he might be able to find a rope or some way of scaling safely to the bottom. In the meantime, he moved a few hay bales around for a make shift bed. As he settled in, Michael considered that as a younger man, he slept in worse circumstances. Of course those were generally after a crazy night of partying, not exploring the mysterious source of dog barking.

*

Lauren laid awake that night wondering if she was dreaming. If it wasn't for the incessant purring of the cat by her side, she may have believed that. However, the occasional hacking of a hairball reminded her that indeed she was in reality. But how did her reality now include a movie star trapped in the hay loft of her barn? And it wasn't any movie star, it was the one she admired when she was younger, one whose career she followed for a long time. One that even Tyler enjoyed. One that was featured in a movie she watched just last week.

Lauren sat up. Did she put away that movie? Was it lying around in the downstairs area, waiting to be discovered? Did she honestly expect that Mick Quinlan was going to be in her living room at some point?

Since stranger things had happened, she got out of her bed and walked downstairs to locate the video. Indeed, it was out on the coffee table, under a coaster with a glass on top that held what remained of melted ice. She picked up the disc and examined the face of Michael Quinlan on the cover. While it was really too dark to know for sure, she speculated that even from the distance, his face held a few more wrinkles than any that were air brushed out of the picture.

As she returned it to the drawer with the other movies, Lauren wondered if there was some way that Tyler could be playing a trick on her. It was exactly the sort of thing he liked to do. However, it was Jim and Alice playing the trick. Why didn't Alice tell her who was staying in Tyler's cabin? Lauren sat on the couch, trying to wrap her mind around all of it. Who else knew he was here? She knew the cabin had a new occupant, and she vowed she would give that person the privacy she herself craved. She wondered if anyone in Kettlesville would even recognize him. His peak of fame was passed and his latest films were somewhat offbeat. While the little town had plenty of quirks, they didn't value it in movie going.

What must it be like to age in the limelight of Hollywood? Two weeks after Tyler died, Lauren found a gray hair and she was mortified. It couldn't be much easier for a man. While she couldn't muster much sympathy for a movie star, Lauren figured she should at least give him an easy escape from her hay loft. After all, she didn't really want to face him first thing in the morning. Neither one of them likely looked very good.

Why did she care what he thought of how she looked anyway?

*

Michael woke to hear dogs panting. He sat up, forgetting where he was. The scratch of the straw quickly reminded him. He heard a soft thud against the ledge of the hay mow and saw the ladder set back to his reach.

Michael put his head back down and closed his eyes. He couldn't help but smile. Maybe getting to know Lauren might be interesting after all.

Chapter Nine–Halt!

The owners walked their dogs in a circle, reversing direction, stopping, putting their dogs in a 'sit,' as Lauren called out commands. After the initial drill was over, they stopped to hear the week's new assignment.

"Our dogs can be like us–barreling along from task to task, without much of a pause. But sometimes your dog may be moving too far, too fast. You want him to pause. That is what the 'halt' command is for. It's a break in the action, if you will. Telling your dog to halt means they stop, usually when they are in motion."

Lauren picked up Guinness' leash and walked him around the inside perimeter of the circle. "You want to give the command while you are still walking, then you stop. As soon as your dog stops, praise him and keep going." Lauren demonstrated and then encouraged the class to give it a try.

After witnessing varying degrees of success, Lauren continued, "Teaching your dog this command is important if he should approach something dangerous or off limits when he is not on leash. Once he stops moving toward the object, you determine whether to sit or release him with an 'ok' if it's safe to proceed."

*

Grocery shopping was something Michael never did. He went from living at home with his parents to caterers on set. He never had those starving artist years or waited a single table. He knew about take-out service from restaurants, and had slipped into a grocery store now and again, but shopping with the intention of preparing meals was not familiar to him. His sister-in-law kindly packed a small box of provisions for him, which he muddled through sufficiently.

Now, however, he craved a meal. There was a bar and diner in town, but he wasn't quite ready for that. Starting with a visit to the grocery store seemed more manageable.

When he drove into the tiny town, he was startled to discover that the grocery store was also the local gas station, which also had a small diner. The cheap sign promised the additional glamour of night crawlers. Michael pulled his car into a haphazard area that served as the parking lot.

Entering the grocery store, two things struck him. One was that there were only three aisles in the store. The other was that the aroma coming from the diner was extremely appetizing. His stomach growled, reminding him a hot meal was in order. The young woman tending the cash register would have been more attractive were it not for the heavy layer of make-up carefully plastered over her face. She gave him a quick smile before shifting her eyes back to the gas pump area where she scrutinized the young man fueling his pickup truck.

A man called from the diner area, "Raylene, we're outta coffee!"

Raylene, the cashier, yelled over her shoulder, "Your arm ain't broke!"

Michael wondered if all those presumptions about small town people being friendly were wrong. As if to prove that point further, Lauren entered the store. She noticed him at the same time as she grabbed a basket. She stopped, the two of them facing each other in a stand-off.

He was taken aback when she turned and disappeared down an aisle. After a moment, he followed her, noticing that she seemed more intent on ignoring him than shopping as she fiddled aimlessly with a jar on a dusty shelf.

"These look delicious," Michael said, snatching the jar from Lauren's hand. "Somehow I never imagined you—or really anyone—buying pig's feet. Tell me, how does one prepare these?"

Lauren took the jar from him and set it back on the shelf. Michael took it back off and put it in his basket. "Oh no. These must be good if you like them."

She glanced in the basket on his arm and removed a gossip tabloid. The front of it read, "Wheel of Misfortune" with a sad Vanna and a delighted Kelly. "You're the last person I thought would buy one of these."

"I never have before, I guess I'm desperate for something to do," Michael grabbed the paper and returned it to his basket. "Thanks for helping me out last night."

Wendy appeared from the end of the aisle, her eyebrows raised at what she'd heard. "Don't let me interrupt." She looked at Lauren and shook her head before moving past.

Lauren quickly moved away and down another aisle, with Michael right behind her. She shot him a look, "Great. Now the whole town will be talking."

"About me?"

"No, about me!" Lauren hissed, "And keep your voice down."

Michael watched as Lauren bought items that actually made sense. It was shaping up to be something like spaghetti sauce so he bought the same items.

She continued to glare at him. "Are you playing a prowler in your next movie, Mr. Quinlan? Is that why you were traipsing around in the barn?"

"You can call me Mickey. I was just curious where all the barking came from."

"Please tell me you're not making a sequel to that detective movie!"

"I see you're familiar with my work. And that did very well," Michael said, then added, "overseas."

He saw the glimmer of a smile on Lauren, "You were trespassing."

"Our mutual neighbor, Franny Bottoms, told me about you." Michael added, "I thought maybe the Dog Lady was a circus sideshow or something."

"I see you're familiar with my work," Lauren shot back at

him, the smile winning. "What else did she tell you about me?"

"What makes you think you were the topic of conversation?"

Lauren stopped in front of what passed as the spice area and gestured around the store, "You have tabloids, I have this."

Michael nodded, "Point taken. This is pretty bottom of the barrel."

Lauren was surprisingly protective, "Hey, this is my barrel you're talking about."

"I can't believe I left sushi for live bait."

"You can leave. It's not like someone has a gun to your head," Lauren said, laughing at her own joke.

Michael frowned, "Very funny. I'm just here to . . ." What was he going to say? He had no script to explain his presence. "To get my head together." He inwardly winced.

Lauren shook her head, "I hate that phrase."

"Me too. It sounds better than getting my head out of my—"

Lauren shot him a look of warning.

Michael realized they were in the produce area. It wasn't big enough to call a section. "Where do they keep the red onions?"

"You want something as exotic as red onions?" Lauren nodded her head toward the cashier, "Ask Raylene."

Michael turned toward her in time to see the woman quickly look down. He hoped she didn't recognize him. He enjoyed the anonymity for a change.

Raylene smiled at Michael, "You new at the college? Whatter ya teachin'?"

"Quantum Physics," Michael answered.

"Kwanza what?" Raylene's brows knit.

"Where are the red onions?" Michael asked hopefully.

This confused Raylene more than his made up profession. She looked over her shoulder at the handwritten sign taped to the wall that had the prices written for potatoes, onions and peppers. "What do they look like?"

Michael paused, waiting for the punch line. When he heard Lauren smother a giggle, he knew he'd been had.

Raylene started laughing too. "You pullin' my leg, ain't you? That is very cute. Red onions." She laughed harder, ending with a definitively unattractive snort.

Michael nodded while he backed away. Turning to find Lauren, he saw her scamper down an aisle. He cornered her by putting up an arm to block her. "You're just a regular laugh riot, you know that?"

He watched Lauren as she became suddenly serious as she stared at his arm. Her playfulness gone, she glared at him before slipping under his arm and returning to the cash register.

As Raylene unloaded Lauren's cart, she chuckled, "Did you hear what that guy said? He asked for red onions. Ain't that the funniest thing you seen all day?"

Lauren grimaced at Raylene's grammar and noticed Michael behind her with the same expression. "Fortunately for you, Raylene, it's still early in the morning. I'm sure something funnier will come along." With a final glare at Michael she added, "It always does."

Lauren picked up her bag, then set it down, pulling out her wallet, "Oh, I need some bags of salt too."

Michael leaned over to say in her ear, "Maybe you should try sugar."

With a toss of her head, Lauren ignored him and exited with her groceries.

As Michael set down his basket, Raylene wagged a finger at him, "Has anyone told you you look like that actor—"

Before she could finish, Michael held up a hand, "Yeah, I get that …"

Raylene finished anyway, "Blake Greer. Only older."

"…A lot," Michael uttered in defeat.

Raylene brightened in agreement, "Yeah, a lot older!"

*

Lauren frowned as she tossed the fourth forty pound bag of softener salt into the back of her pickup truck. She shouldn't be jarred by something like a man's muscular arm, yet she was. At one time Tyler was strong. He loaded the bags of salt two at a time. Over the years, the disease sapped his strength. Perhaps she simply forgot what a normal man looked like. Not that she described Michael as normal on any level. For one thing he was extremely handsome.

Just then Michael exited the store. He set his bag down, "Here, let me give you a hand."

Lauren reached for another bag, "So help me if you start applauding I'll throw this on you."

"Let me help you," Michael took the bag from her hands and tossed it in with the others. He made it look easy, which greatly annoyed her.

"Stop! I've got it," Lauren said.

Michael tossed a few more bags into her truck while waving her off, "Just accept some help, would you?"

Lauren folded her arms and leaned against the tailgate and watched Michael work. "Suit yourself."

After throwing in several more bags, he stopped and panted, "Now see? That wasn't so hard. How many do you need?" The back of her truck sagged.

"Five."

"Oh," Michael said, turning to look at the bags he'd loaded. Sheepishly, he unloaded half the bags.

When he finished, he dusted off his hands and looked down at his now dirty jeans. He walked up close to Lauren, "Why don't you like me?"

Lauren looked him in the eye, feeling again that distressing stirring. The face she mooned over twenty years ago was a foot away from hers. Quickly, she turned and hopped into the driver's seat of the truck. After she shut the door, she leaned out the window and called to him, "Who says I don't like you?"

As she pulled away, she snuck a quick glance in the rear view mirror. A small cloud of dust swirled around him from her tires. Lauren smiled. That was fun.

*

When she got home, Alice and Jim's car was in the driveway. Part of her wanted to let them both have it for not telling her that Tyler's cabin was occupied by Michael Quinlan. But she knew they were at her house to help her carry the water softener salt bags to her basement. Considering how rickety her staircase was, she could hardly be angry at them when they risked their life to help her.

As Jim and Alice disappeared up the back porch with salt bags heaved over their shoulders, Lauren reached for one, just as Michael steered into the driveway.

Guinness ran to the car and nosed Michael as he got out carrying a casserole dish. Lauren recognized it immediately. "Leave it!"

"Don't worry, I'm not going to help you," Michael said.

"I've got friends helping me."

"You've got friends?" Michael dropped his jaw in mock surprise. Then he got serious, "They won't make a big deal when they see me, will they?"

Lauren paused. "Don't worry. They're hippies. They won't even know who you are."

Michael looked as if he would reply when Alice stepped out the back door. Lauren quickly added, "I'll introduce you to Firefly Redbeans and her husband, Conky. But keep in mind they are hard of hearing."

Michael looked at her, "And I thought the name Franny Bottoms was bad."

Alice approached and called out, "Hi there!"

Michael set the casserole dish on the hood of his car and extended his hand to Alice. He yelled, "Hi Mrs. Redbeans! I'm Mickey!"

Alice's hand went still in Michael's grip. "What?"

Michael yelled louder, "Sorry, do you go by Firefly?"

Jim joined the group and Michael enthusiastically yelled, "Hi Conky! I'm –"

Jim shook his hand and said calmly, "You're Mick Quinlan. I'm Jim, Tom's brother. Why are you yelling?"

Finally finding her voice, Alice asked, "You two know each other?"

"Alice, this is Tom's friend, Mick Quinlan. Also Lauren's tenant."

Clearly there was no name recognition for Alice. "How do you know Tom?"

Jim, Lauren, and Michael all stared at Alice.

Michael said, "We're both in entertainment."

Lauren butted in, "Yes, Mickey's an exotic dancer."

Alice looked Michael up and down, "Oh."

Jim laughed, the only one to do so, "Lauren!"

Alice looked around confusedly, "Why did you call me Firefly?"

Unable to keep her face straight anymore, Lauren burst out laughing. Michael glared and Alice remained confused.

Jim showed his true kindness, "Mick, come by the college for a tour. Auditions are in a week for our summer stock show."

"A week?" Michael asked.

Jim laughed, "I know. What will you do with yourself for that long? Don't worry. Time passes in unusual ways around here."

Michael nodded and looked sideways at Lauren, "I've noticed that."

After Jim chatted with Michael a bit longer, he and Alice were in their car and ready to leave. Lauren clung to the window on Alice's side. "Are you sure you guys have to go?"

"Yeah, it's time for the Red Beans to go home." Jim shook his head at her, "That's the first joke I've heard you make in a long time, Lauren."

As they began to back out of the driveway, Lauren heard Alice say to Jim, "I didn't know Tom represented exotic dancers."

Lauren watched them leave, waiting until the last moment to

face Michael. She expected the worst. When she did finally turn around, Michael was standing at the foot of her back porch, noting the ramp.

"Is that so you can get a running start on your broom?"

Before Lauren could snap at him, Guinness jumped on the hood of Michael's car. Scout growled and jumped at the side of it.

Michael yelled, "My car!"

"My dogs!" Lauren waved the dogs off as Michael grabbed the casserole dish. "Are you trying to poison my dogs?"

"No, I was trying to make friends with them. I thought someone around here should think I'm a good and decent person."

"Poisoning them with Franny Bottoms' cooking isn't the way," Lauren sighed.

"How did you know it was from her?"

"She makes that stuff by the cauldron." She turned away from him and called the dogs, who raced to her side and followed.

Michael followed as well, "I'm beginning to understand why you're single."

Lauren stopped and turned to face him, "You'll have to excuse me, I have class."

"I'm not saying you don't."

Lauren let a small giggle escape. "No, I mean I have

obedience class."

Michael's crinkled brow made her explain further, "For dogs."

Lynne E. Scott

Chapter Ten—Those Big Brown Eyes

Michael followed Lauren into the training space of the kennel building. He rubbed Guinness' ears while owners and dogs arrived and took their spot in the large circle with Lauren in the middle. Franny Bottoms came in late, hobbling in on her cane with Goliath. She waved enthusiastically at Michael as he sat off to the side. Normally he'd avoid someone like Franny, but she made him smile and he waved back with what he hoped was equal fervor.

Guinness zipped to Lauren when she called him and for the next hour he never took his eyes off of her. Michael watched the dog's dedication. Clearly he hung on her every word.

After a few drills, Lauren got to the lesson for the day. "True discipline is controlled behavior. Mrs. Bottoms—"

"Lauren, for Pete's sake, call me Franny." She pointed her cane at the other people, "Everyone knows me."

Without skipping a beat, Lauren smiled politely and continued. "You said Goliath barks at you often throughout the day. What do you do when he barks at you?"

"I give him a treat." Franny said. "That's the only thing that makes him stop."

"Until he wants another treat, right?" Lauren asked. "He has you trained very well."

From the class' response, it was clear Franny Bottoms was not the only person who was guilty of this scenario.

Lauren leaned down and patted Goliath, "He's awfully cute. Have you always been a sucker for those big brown eyes?"

Franny giggled, "He pretty much gets what he wants."

Guinness followed Lauren as she stood up and walked around the circle, "To some extent, we all spoil our dogs. Let's face it, it's one of the things we enjoy about them. The difference is when it turns into the dog running the owner's life and not the other way around, there's no reason for a dog to listen to their owner. They don't respect the person who gives into their demands all the time. When we resist the dog's insistence to do it his way and instead make the dog earn the reward, then the dog will respect us and depend on us more. Then we can teach the dog lots of different things—which will ultimately make for a safer environment for the dog and a happier home for the adults. Don't forget, strength comes through resistance."

After class ended, the owners filed out with their dogs. Michael began to approach Lauren when a shout interrupted them, and one of the dog owners called for her. At the edge of the building, Franny was on the ground, Goliath almost under her.

"I fell on the leash," Franny said, but with a good-natured smile.

"Did you trip?" Lauren helped the woman up, while Michael stood at the side, clearly unsure of what to do to help.

"No, I was a bit wobbly and grabbed for something to steady me. So I grabbed at that plant stand. Turns out it wasn't so steady either."

"Franny, I'm sorry," Lauren dusted off the hem of Franny's loud housedress.

Franny took it in stride, "You know, Tyler promised me a handrail at my house. Could use one here too."

"Yeah, well, Tyler promised a lot of things he couldn't do." Lauren said. By Franny's questioning look, Lauren realized she'd been too flip in her response. She said quietly, "You know, he just ran out of time." She mentally kicked herself. What was worse was Michael standing there listening to the whole thing.

After everyone left, Lauren's mood was dark. Oblivious, Michael followed her into the kennel area and poured water for the dogs as Lauren fed them. He joked about the dogs to her, and his cajoling seemed to warm her. Then he did an impersonation of her ordering the dog owners around that made her double over with laughter.

"Did you learn anything?" Lauren said when she caught her breath.

Michael nodded, "Much. Most of all, I think I learned I dated Goliath. I'm a sucker for those big brown eyes."

"At least you know which end of the leash you're on. That's step one."

Seeing that she was in a good mood, Michael decided to push her a bit. "It's Saturday night. That's date night, you know."

Lauren turned her back as she reached for a bag of food, "I'm not interested."

Michael matched her tone, "I'm not asking. But I'd like to get out."

Lauren raised an eyebrow at him, "There's a word for immature pleasure seekers."

"Happy?" Michael suggested.

"Hedonists. You should try living in the real world for a while." Lauren laughed, scooped the dog food into a bowl and slid it into a kennel run. After she closed the gate, she secured the latch with a clip.

"You're just a regular laugh riot, aren't you? Seems awful dull. Did you and this Tyler guy ever have any fun?"

Lauren's laugh died as she turned to face him. Her hand absently closed the gate on a young Rottweiler that hopped excitedly at the banter. "Tell me you didn't just say that."

"I'm sorry—I was just kidding around," Michael held his hands up. "Franny didn't give me details."

Lauren stared at him, "I can't believe this."

"It's been a year. Surely you've had some stud muffin to

keep you warm at night." Michael knew his flippant remark went too far as soon as the words came out.

"Get out." Lauren said, too calmly.

Instead of sensibly listening to her, he pushed on, "Just be honest. Tell me about him."

Lauren took a step forward, pointing at the door, "Are you insane? Stop it!"

"C'mon. Did he sweep you off your feet?"

"Get out!" Lauren's voice raised.

"Tell me what happened!" Michael shouted back.

The latch of the Rottweiler's cage flipped open. The dog raced straight toward Michael and planted his front two paws squarely on his chest, knocking him backward against another kennel run.

"Brutus, leave it!"

When the dog refused to leave Michael, she tackled the dog and they both slid to the ground. Brutus turned and licked Lauren's face, his bobbed tail wagging. Lauren sat up and held the dog's collar as it again faced Michael.

"I'm not sure if I'm relieved or amazed," Michael said, panting.

Lauren stood and said flatly, "I suggest you go home and decide."

As he slowly got up, he quietly said, "Just tell me who Tyler was."

Lauren stroked the ears of the dog and led it back to the kennel cage. As she latched the gate, she met Michael's eyes. "He was my husband. He died. Now leave."

Michael turned toward the door. He glanced back over his shoulder just as he reached the door. Lauren was still glaring at him. The hurt in her eye was much greater than the anger. Maybe he'd blown it completely, but it was an old habit of his to try levity, "Alright, I'll go. But I do so with my tail between my legs!"

He turned and walked out the door. He thought he heard a snort of laughter. Maybe it was the dog, maybe it was Lauren. He hoped he made her laugh. But why did he care about that?

That evening, Michael attempted to put together one of the puzzles he found in the closet. It kept his thoughts semi-occupied. He kept thinking of Lauren. He thought of what else was in that closet, things that belonged to her husband. Her sainted, dead husband. How could he compete with that? He fell far short of him, that much was clear. If he had to think about it much more thoroughly, he was confident he fell far short of most honorable men.

Looking down at the puzzle pieces he was able to complete so far, he saw only a portion of the edge. He looked at the scattered pieces all around him, yet to be assembled. The sun was coming up. This was the result–an unfinished puzzle. He knocked the lid to the floor and crawled onto the couch, his back aching.

*

The evening was no better for Lauren. She huddled in the

corner of her couch, staring at the blank television. How could he have said those things? Was it really so out of the ordinary not to jump from relationship to relationship? Didn't people take any time to absorb and examine their pain? And no matter his accusations, the thought of having a fling repulsed her. Intimacy was earned.

Why did he badger her so? While she didn't know him well, no decent person would push her like that. What did he want? And why couldn't she let it go?

Pulling Ty's shirt over her shoulders closer, she looked down at the puzzle she'd completed over the last couple of hours. She thought of how Tyler teased her about her obsession with them. Once she started one, she couldn't stop. Nothing else would get done. Of course, Lauren preferred a small puzzle, one that she could solve in a short period of time. Challenges beyond that–ones that took too much time–were to be avoided.

Lynne E. Scott

Chapter Eleven–Mistake or Misdirection

Wendy fussed with Sparky as the owners went through their paces. "Martin never has this problem!" Eventually, Sparky laid down and looked at his owner. "Why does he do that?"

Lauren took the leash from her and walked Sparky to the center. "It's common for one member of the household to have more of a problem with the dog than another." From the mutterings in the group, Lauren knew she was right. "We all communicate differently to each other, and that includes how we communicate obedience commands to our dogs."

Sparky followed Lauren as she slow jogged around the group, weaving in and out, as well as changing directions. She gave him various commands, most of which he followed with ease. When he didn't, Lauren calmly corrected the dog and lavished praise on Sparky when he got it right. "Sometimes the dog makes mistakes. The key is not to act like it's a big deal. Show them the correct way, then move on from there. When we get frustrated, then we aren't clearly directing him. Then the dog gets confused and responds as Sparky did–lying flat until he understands what is expected of him. Please throw perfectionism out the window. None of us can live up to that and neither can your dog."

After the owners left, Michael entered the kennel building and found Lauren at her desk. He placed his peace offering in front of her, which took up nearly all the space. "I'm sorry for being a jerk."

"Flowers?" Lauren parted some of the fronds so she could see Michael. "I've never seen an arrangement, uh, quite this elaborate."

"I asked the florist for the biggest one they could make." Michael sat, proud of himself. Realizing Lauren was hidden from view, he stood back up.

Lauren frowned, "Did you go to the florist in town?"

"Sure did—buy local, right?" he beamed. Hearing her sigh, he tried to rally her, "Honestly, there's some real talent there. I'm not just saying that."

"Oh, they are talented all right. They are also Tyler's cousins." Lauren moved the flowers to a side table, taking the tiny card from it and reading the brief note to her. "But it's the thought that counts, no matter what the gossip fallout."

Michael shrunk. "Of all people, I should have thought of that. Perhaps I should have gone with the on-line fruit on a stick apology instead?"

Lauren grinned despite herself, "I'd hate to think what would arrive if you were going all out with cost there."

"At least an entire pineapple," Michael raised an eyebrow at her.

Shaking her head, Lauren stood up and went to the mini

fridge, "Let's move on. Want a bottle of water? Sorry it's not imported."

Michael looked as surprised by her offer as she did at making it. Opening his, he tapped hers, "To forgiveness."

The rest of the evening continued with more surprises of pleasant, easy going conversation. Maybe neither of them had any more energy to argue. Or maybe they were starting to enjoy each other.

*

The next day, Michael finally had something to do–a place to go–and people to see. He woke up energized. He went to the drive-thru part of the gas station and ordered a coffee. He was so excited he forgot how terrible it was.

While his expectations were low, he still was eager to get out to see Jim's little theater. The college was small, yet fit in with the nearby town well. It was a quick five minute drive to the theater from his cabin. Who knew he was so close to semi-civilization? He sat in the parking lot sipping his coffee and looked at the building. It was newer than he expected.

What would his life have been like if he went to college instead of going into acting? It was hard for him to regret not going when his career had been successful. Did he just think the words "had been?"

He got out of the car and entered the vast lobby. Walking into the auditorium of the theater, he was further impressed. Jim was on stage working with a handful of students. One of the young women recognized Michael immediately as she elbowed a young man and pointed. Michael was both startled and pleased. He was still relevant with the younger generation after all.

Jim instructed the group to take a break and he stepped down to greet Michael. "Not a bad setup for a little fly-over state, is it?"

Michael looked up at the ceiling, noticing some details, "It's not what I expected."

"Nothing here is. Let me give you a quick tour." Jim walked him down a corridor that featured large framed photos of previous productions.

"Tom said you were doing a retro festival or something this summer?"

Jim laughed, "Retro is one way of putting it. We're doing short plays–over a hundred years old."

"At least they're older than me."

Jim stopped, "It would be great to have your help. Your experience and perspective would greatly enhance their education in this field. So many students have wild ideas of what stardom is like."

Michael smirked, "I'd hate to spoil their wide-eyed wonder. It doesn't last long enough." He noticed a photo on the poster behind Jim. "Is that Lauren?"

Jim turned, "It sure is. She was pretty active in the program when she was here."

"You mean she used to be fun?"

"From what I hear from the older professors she was also talented."

Michael shook his head, examining the picture of a much younger Lauren, "Why didn't she do something significant?"

Jim frowned, "Some might say marrying Tyler was plenty significant. Despite how things worked out, I doubt she'd change her life."

Michael felt the same sick feeling he got from antagonizing her. Eager to switch the subject, he said, "If I helped you, what would you want me to do?"

Jim smiled and the two returned to the auditorium.

*

When Michael returned to his cabin, he felt antsy again. He wasn't sure about the theater thing. It likely would demand more of him than he could reliably deliver. After all, he wasn't technical and had no experience doing any actual teaching. How did someone learn to teach? He thought of how Lauren confidently taught the dog classes. Lauren. He didn't want to think about her. He needed to get out of here. It was a stupid idea to come to this nowhere land.

Michael took out the old guitar in the back of the closet and strummed it, seeing how far out of tune it might be. At one time he played often. That was a long time ago. His place was in front of the camera. What would he do with a bunch of overly ambitious college students?

Desperate, he called Tom and asked if there was any possible work for him. The news wasn't promising.

"Celebrity Flab Camp called. They want you and that one guy from the Beastie Boys."

"No way, I was in rehab with that guy. Besides, I'm not flabby." Michael walked to the mirror and lifted his shirt, poking his surprisingly flabby belly. *When did this happen?*

"Jim said you were going to 'think about' helping him. I know that means you don't want to. What's up?"

Michael sighed. That didn't take long to get to Tom. "I wanted something cutting edge. They are doing *Our Town* and *She Stoops to Conquer*."

"Really, Mick, are you too good to focus on the classics? You would enjoy them." Tom's voice seemed to have an edge Michael didn't recognize.

"Do you have any alternatives?"

Over the phone, he heard Tom sigh, "Anthony Andrews pulled out of an historical."

"Where's it being filmed?"

"Newfoundland."

"Nope." Michael was in no mood to be hearty. Not yet.

"Right. When I find the lead for a thriller based in Grand Cayman, I'll let you know," said Tom before signing off.

Michael picked up the copy of the play, "*She Stoops to Conquer.*" Unable to focus his attention, he flipped on the radio.

The voice of an older woman began to read a recipe, word for word, ingredient for ingredient, with long pauses for a person to write it down. It was agonizing. Yet Michael kept listening. It was a voice, and it was also strangely comforting.

The disc jockey interrupted, "We hope you enjoyed our recipe show. Now everyone can make a refreshing lemonade pie. Sounds good in this heat, doesn't it?"

Michael broke down and rummaged through the last box in the closet. He knew it was some of Tyler's personal items. But he was desperate. He found a well-worn Bible, a piece of yellowed newspaper sticking out. He opened it to find an article from the paper about their wedding. Lauren looked radiant. Tyler clearly adored her.

It was too much. Michael carefully closed the Bible, set it back in the box, and pushed it toward the back where he found it. He sat on the ground and stared at the closet. What did he expect to find by going through someone's personal belongings? It wasn't hard to think of it as treading on holy ground. Michael grimaced.

He got up and sunk onto the couch. For over half his life, he was insulated from the real world. For years he thought he was worldly and experienced. He rubbed elbows with some of the best directors and actors in the world. He went to top political events. He read erudite books.

Yet it was an illusion. His world was only a bubble. If his peers got sick or even got old, most quietly left the industry. Perhaps he had a fleeting moment of sadness at the misfortunes of others, but all were at a distance. Suffering for him until now consisted of gas station coffee.

People living in the real world had everyday problems.

People experienced tragedies and didn't collapse in heaps, become mass murderers, or sail off into the sunset with their life perfectly restored. What he was learning from Lauren was that most people lived somewhere in the middle.

Chapter Twelve–Controlling the Head and Heart

Lauren woke up groggy. What she wouldn't give to sleep longer on this dreary morning. Plus, she was confounded by her own thoughts, which constantly gravitated toward Michael, even though she willed them not to. And, as had been the case for over a week, he was on her mind when she woke.

Sleeping in was never an option when there were dogs in the kennel waiting to go out. The two sets of eyes staring at her as she opened her own were a reminder that her own dogs were eager to go out. Not for the first time, she was thankful for the kennel forcing her out of bed in the morning.

As she made her way into the kennel, she noticed a rail along the steps. She ran her hand over it and checked its sturdiness. It would hold Franny Bottoms if she took another tumble. But where had it come from? Jim wasn't handy.

In one of her recent conversations with Michael, he mentioned having minor manual labor skills. Every now and then he did surprise her in good ways. She found she was eager to see him and thank him. Again her thoughts betrayed her as she thought about hugging him, and not stopping at hugging.

Kissing. Yes. Kissing. Hmm….when was the last time she thought about kissing?

"Stop it!" she yelled. Scout stopped and sat down, looking at Lauren for permission to proceed. "It's not you, it's me." She said to the dog. She sighed and patted his head as Guinness came running to join them. "I just need more coffee," she sighed.

When Lauren walked back into the house, the phone was ringing. She glanced at the time–seven thirty in the morning. Fortunately, she was plenty awake to answer.

"Hi, we're starting your next session of obedience classes and wondered what you thought about these halter things some dogs wear. My wife just freaks out when she sees those choke collars."

Lauren poured herself some coffee and sat down, "Your wife isn't alone, but they can be used properly with great results. The head halters are great, though it often takes the dog additional time to adjust."

"Aren't they for horses? I told her I think they look dumb." The man sounded impatient, which likely was due to the sound of his wife's voice in the background peppering him with questions.

Lauren smiled to herself. Sometimes she missed that part of a relationship, in a strange sort of way. "The head halter has a strap that goes over the dog's snout and one behind the head. When the dog receives a correction or runs too far ahead, the straps tighten and the dog stops. They can be very effective."

Suddenly, the wife's voice was on the phone, "It doesn't hurt them? It sounds like it hurts them."

Lauren rolled her eyes, thankful she couldn't be seen, "It may be a momentary discomfort. But I think you can live with that if it means your dog listens to you. Just remember, when you control the dog's head, you control his heart."

*

Michael woke with thoughts of Lauren. However, he often thought about whatever woman he saw as potential companions. Lauren wasn't like them. For one thing, he enjoyed her company. He often thought about things to discuss with her, and she proved a worthy conversationalist, often bantering with him, bringing up other points of view, challenging him. In his world, most everyone thought the same thing. If you dared to question something, a person could be quickly ostracized. While it was nice to have a peer group that looked past a lot of bad behavior, challenging the status quo was not tolerated. Lauren was a breath of fresh air.

A knock on the door got him on his feet. He heard the yipping of a dog. A tiny dog. He opened the door to a smiling Franny Bottoms. Before he could properly focus his bleary eyes, she forced a casserole dish into his hands.

"Thought you'd like some more chicken casserole. The last one was licked clean!" She chortled.

"Not again," Michael muttered.

Franny tilted her head to the side, "What's that, Son?"

"It's going to be hot again," he said loudly. "It's really been a long heat wave, hasn't it?"

When Franny pushed her way inside, he noticed her foot was bandaged. He set the casserole dish in the kitchen and motioned for her to sit down. Didn't anyone sleep past nine in the morning around here?

"Your kids must appreciate your cooking. Maybe they would enjoy this? Maybe they have kids to feed?" Michael persisted hopefully. Really, anything to not have this smelly casserole in his house again.

Franny set her foot up on an opposite chair. She was making herself too much at home for Michael's comfort. She was nice enough, but this wasn't how he saw his day going. Of course, he really had no plans for anything for her to interrupt.

"All I have left is a grandson. He lives in Washington, D.C. He's an intern there, can you believe it?"

Michael shook his head, "No, I really can't."

Their attention was drawn to Goliath, who was digging at the cushions of the couch. Franny picked up the newspaper on the table and shook it at Goliath. "Goliath! Leave it! Leave it!"

The dog ignored her. Franny looked at Michael, "I'm helpless. I told Lauren I gotta quit taking Goliath to school 'cuz of my ankle." She looked Michael straight in the eye, "Unless I find someone to take him for me."

As she stared at him expectantly, Michael weighed his options. Stay at home and never complete a tedious jigsaw puzzle or help Franny.

"I guess I could spend more time with her. I mean him—Goliath is a him," Michael quickly corrected himself. With her poor hearing, he figured she didn't catch that. From the smile that crept across Franny's face, he realized maybe she did.

*

Lauren returned from the kennel in a happy mood. She turned on the radio, but changed the station promptly after hearing another devastating world event. Every morning she woke up and listened to the news. It didn't exactly set a good tone for the rest of the day. While she liked to keep informed, too much talk was too much aggravation. She found the local radio station. While she disliked a lot of the musical selections, she appreciated that it was locally owned and not a slave to the formatting demands of syndication. The disc jockeys were local people who talked about local things. What they lacked in sophistication, they made up in warmth.

A song came on that she and her friends used to dance to at college parties. She abandoned the dishes to dance across the kitchen. The dogs hopped around her, sensing her lighter mood. Working up a sweat, she took off Ty's shirt that was over her T-shirt. She danced with abandon as she remembered what it was like then to dance to this song. Without any cares. She remembered that feeling. And when the song ended, she remembered what it was like to live in the real world, the time beyond college.

She sighed and returned to the dishes.

Lynne E. Scott

Chapter Thirteen–Fighting the Leash

Lauren greeted the dogs and owners as they entered the building, checking off the names on her clipboard. By this time, she knew most of them and could keep track, but she really liked to see it in front of her. There was just something so comforting about order.

Goliath's yip surprised Lauren, but not as much as seeing Michael holding the leash. Lauren frowned at him. "What are you doing?"

"I have class," Michael answered.

Lauren looked down at her clipboard, "That's debatable."

"I have dog class," he smirked.

Franny bellowed her friendly, "Hellloooo!" and grabbed the handrail as she carefully made her way up the steps, "Mickey's going to help me train Goliath. Isn't that nice of him, Lauren?"

Lauren glanced back at Michael. "He's a real charmer, Franny." She motioned to the group with her pen, "Join the circle."

As Michael hopped over Goliath's leash as the dog darted around his feet, Lauren suppressed a smile. This might be a fun class after all. She went to the middle of the group and instructed the class to begin with some laps around the circle.

"Remember, the dog should be heeling by your side," She watched the group and made comments where she saw fit. "By this time, your dog should know this one. Velma, don't let Skipper pull you–pop him back into place. Good!"

She watched as the owner of a Basset hound who lagged behind his owner encouraged the dog forward. "Here, Mr. Durbin, take these treats and put them down on his level. Pat your leg to get him moving faster and you walk faster too. Don't adjust to his pace. He adjusts to yours!"

Goliath's yip permeated the room. Lauren looked over to see the little dog lunging at the back end of the Basset hound. Michael pulled the dog back but as soon as he loosened the leash, the dog lunged again.

"Reverse!" Lauren said loudly.

The owners all turned around, with most dogs doing the same. Almost bumping into someone, Michael turned to walk the other direction, now dragging Goliath as he snapped at the Basset hound's nose.

"Walk faster, Michael. Don't let your dog be nasty to Walter!"

"He is not my dog," Michael muttered in an accent reminiscent of a Peter Sellers' movie.

Lauren couldn't help it as a bit of laughter escaped her. She shook her head and wagged a finger at him, "Pink Panther Movie. Now get moving."

Michael looked over at Walter the Basset hound, whose sad face looked even sadder as he pulled his head back to avoid the lunging Yorkshire terrier. He walked faster, forcing Goliath to keep up. Eventually, the dog forgot about the dog behind him and saw Scout standing in the middle by Lauren.

Goliath shot sideways, wrapping his leash around Michael's long legs. Michael tripped and when he took a step sideways, he landed square on Goliath's tiny foot. The dog screamed bloody murder and howled.

Michael uttered an expletive and unwrapped himself from the leash. Lauren took the leash from him and lifted Goliath up. "He's fine," she announced to the class. "Go forward, then circle and keep going." As the class moved forward, she looked at Michael, "I've got an idea for this guy." She removed a small head harness and fitted it carefully around Goliath's head.

Lauren set the dog down and started moving with the class as Goliath tried to remove the halter with his front paws. Moving faster, the dog needed all four legs to keep up with her, and the halter stayed in place. Every now and then the dog would screech and hop to dig at the harness.

Michael joined Franny and sat to watch Lauren. Franny wrung her hands and looked at Michael, "Do you think she's hurting him?" Franny, not being a quiet person, was unaware that everyone in the class heard her question.

Lauren looked over at them both as she trotted around with Goliath fighting her, "We can't indulge his dramatics. He's just not happy that he's not in control." She caught Michael's eye, "This dog is really quite an actor."

She turned her head with a smile, but not before she caught Michael's smirk. The class was tiring, "Halt!" The dogs and owners screeched to a stop, "Have your dog sit and walk out in front of him and practice the 'stay' command."

As the owners did this, Lauren kept working with Goliath. The little dog was watching her as she turned abruptly or reversed directions. It was as if he forgot about this new torment on his head. She slowed her pace on the next circle and Goliath walked quietly at her left side, in exactly the correct position.

By this time, the class was engrossed in Goliath's behavior. Lauren reversed directions one more time, but slowed even farther. Goliath was panting, but watched her every move. When Lauren stopped, the little dog sat perfectly. What was more, he stayed there, looking up at her, waiting for her next move.

Franny clapped with delight. The class joined in. Michael shook his head and smiled at her.

She smiled back and then looked around at the class. "Knowing that Goliath wasn't hurt, I ignored his shrieks of protest. If you rescue your dog from every imagined pain, you are not going to have a very hearty dog. A little trouble can be a good thing."

*

"No one misses me," Michael said to absolutely no one.

As he sat on the back porch drinking an ordinary cup of coffee, he pondered the cornfields around him. It took him a long time to get used to the absence of noise and distraction, but after several weeks of being in this cabin he could finally sit for several minutes without feeling antsy. While a stray breeze might stir the corn stalks rustling, he often sat quietly. It was the most relaxed he felt for years, maybe even decades.

That's when he realized that no one missed him. Tom, his agent, wasn't calling. His brother checked in with him after his first week in Kettlesville but hadn't bothered since then. Of course, this wasn't his brother's fault. Michael rarely checked in with anyone, always bouncing from project to project and woman to woman when there were gaps. The few friends he had were involved in their own lives. Yet it was odd not to be missed beyond a random text. He was not news on the gossip shows or papers. He knew he should feel thankful for the latter. Mostly what he felt was self-pity.

"Poor little movie star," he muttered, again to no one. Was he so insignificant to most people in his life? The more he thought about it, he wondered who he was missing. No one. What he was missing was attention. Pathetic.

Guinness trotted from around the path through the cornfield. He sprang onto the porch and wagged his tail to greet Michael. The dog found a tennis ball on the porch and grabbed it in his mouth. He stood in front of Michael, staring him down, waiting for the game to begin.

"What do you want?" Michael teased. The dog didn't move, his ears perked, expectant. "Fine."

Michael leaned down and eased the ball from the dog's

mouth. He stood and threw it across the yard, toward the path. Just then Lauren appeared, tossing up an arm just in time to avoid being hit.

"Hey!" Lauren yelled. Without missing a beat, the dog scooped up the ball, raced in a wide arc, then dropped it at Lauren's feet. She picked it up and threw it back at Michael.

Michael apologized profusely as Lauren approached the porch. Fortunately, she was in a good mood. "You learn to throw in a baseball movie or something?"

Michael threw the ball again for Scout. "Believe it or not, I had a very short time in high school sports. I was the best outfielder our team ever had."

"Wow. That seems so normal."

Michael shrugged, "Yeah, I was normal for a while. Now I talk to myself in the middle of the cornfield."

Lauren grinned and sat down across from Michael at the little table. "Don't worry. Around here that's perfectly normal."

"Do you talk to yourself?"

"I do, but I pretend I'm talking to the animals. I mean, I realized I wasn't talking much at all. Then one day, I was watching college football. Next thing I know, I'm yelling at the television. It startled the dogs and scared one of the cats right out of the room. I realized that since Tyler died, they hardly heard the sound of a human voice. So I started talking to them more."

Michael looked at Lauren a bit longer. "That actually makes

sense. But I don't think it makes sense for me to be doing it."

Lauren leaned forward, "Michael, it's okay to be lonely. It won't be a permanent condition."

Michael shrugged. Admitting to loneliness seemed to admit to abject failure. "You get lonely out here, too?"

"Of course. Everyone gets lonely," She gave him a long look. "Whether they admit to it or not."

He grinned back, "You must really miss your husband."

Lauren's expression was lighter than he expected, "I could never wish him back in the state he was in. And sometimes I felt lonely when I was married too. Tyler probably did too. I think everyone does."

Michael nodded, "Whether they admit to it or not." He downed the last of his coffee. "So why are you here?"

Lauren shrugged indifferently, then shot him a smile, "I missed you."

Michael felt a warming in his chest. "I doubt that," he smiled.

"And thanks for the hand rail for Franny. That was needed for a long time," Lauren smiled gently.

The two of them sat quietly, watching Guinness and Scout chase each other before coming up to the porch for some rest. As they panted, Lauren got up.

"Guess I better get these guys some water. Enjoy your day."

Michael watched Lauren and the dogs disappear down the

path. Enjoy his day. That was a tall order.

With a full day of nothing unfolding before him, Michael's resolve to stay away from gossip weakened so he checked a celeb site on his phone. It was one of the rattier, low brow ones, but at least their headlines were entertaining.

He squinted at the screen. That couldn't be right. He quickly turned on his laptop and tapped his foot anxiously until it sprung to life. He clicked around until he found what he was looking for. He gasped as he read the link to Kelly's blog post, "Mickey Quinlan, put out to pasture."

"How does she know I'm here?" he muttered as he read the rest. Somehow she'd managed to become popular enough for the websites to link her blog to their headlines. From the picture of Kelly, he saw from her low cut top that she finally got the surgery she wanted so badly. He glanced through the article, noting her offhand comment about him. The rest was her bragging about "a certain little fling with Chet Davis" she was enjoying. He hesitated, but a sick curiosity took over and he played the video she linked. Mostly it was more bragging. At least her grammar was improved.

"And finally, don't forget my new book, *Proven Winner: Lessons to Get You to the Top*. It's everything I learned to get me where I am now. Five thousand downloads in the first day. Thanks, Guys!"

He wondered if anyone would come looking for him in this town. He wasn't sure which scenario he hoped for. He wanted to be left alone out here, but not being pursued meant he wasn't newsworthy. As with so many things in his profession, there was no winning. Michael reached for his phone and called Tom.

"Did you forget about the time zone thing, Mick?" Tom's grumpy voice asked.

Michael glanced at the clock, admitting that he had and apologized. When he asked Tom about Kelly's knowledge of his whereabouts, Tom had no answers.

"It could be anyone these days, Mick." Tom sounded more awake, "So, I hear you've been going toe to toe with a certain neighbor?"

"She won't let me get that close," Michael flippantly answered. "You and Jim must really enjoy talking about us."

"Oh, there's an 'us'?" Tom teased.

"You're worse than the gossips. Forget that. Is there any news for me?"

He heard Tom sigh, "Blake Greer got the thriller you asked about."

Michael shot off the couch and paced, "Blake Greer? He's a child. He can't handle a role that demands maturity."

"It gets worse," Tom said, "They are calling him the new Mick Quinlan."

Michael sank back on the couch. He almost dropped the phone, "What does that make me?" Tom, to his credit, didn't respond. Michael mumbled something and ended the call. He knew what it made him. Old was the shortest four letter word in Hollywood.

Somehow, he frittered away the rest of the day, though he now understood the true meaning of cabin fever. He had to get out, even if it was finally getting dark. As he walked out the back door, he knew exactly where he was going. The path through the cornfield at twilight was creepy. He thought of horror movies. Right now, nothing scared him more than his fading career and aging body.

The light from the kennel was on. As Michael approached, he could see Lauren in the window. He stopped to watch as she crouched at the entrance of an open kennel run. In the back of it a small dog cowered, its ears flattened against its head.

While he knew he shouldn't spy, he couldn't quite tear himself away from the scene. Lauren turned her head away from the dog and sat, reaching her hand out to the dog. The dog crawled toward her like a commando and sniffed her hand. Lauren didn't move as it nudged her hand and took a bit of food before racing back to its corner.

Michael couldn't hear what she was saying to the dog, but she continued to look away as she talked. The dog carefully approached again, this time licking her hand. Lauren smiled and continued to talk. Soon the dog cuddled up in her lap, its tiny tail wagging. Lauren now looked at the dog and petted it. The little tail wagged faster as it reached to lick her face.

Michael stepped away from the window. He didn't want her to see him. Maybe he should go in and say hello, like he planned. However, he didn't want to interrupt her work with the little dog. Sometimes she made training look so simple. Yet he knew from his brief hour with Goliath that fear can turn to aggression quickly.

Panting behind him startled Michael from his thoughts. Guinness wagged his tail at him. "Hey, Big Guy. At least I've got one loyal friend." The dog scooped up a stick and walked away to sit under a tree. "You're waiting for Lauren too, huh?" He remembered what Lauren said about dogs not being big on conversation.

He sat under the tree and scratched the dog behind his ears. The dog chewed the stick into mulch. Michael thought about Kelly and wondered if he would ever want a woman like that again. There was nothing about her that was real, even though she was a beauty. While Lauren didn't share the same physical characteristics of most starlets, there was definitely something about her that was more attractive. She didn't seem fazed by his celebrity status and talked to him like a real person. If he were honest, he wouldn't mind if she would act a little more dazzled by him. He had the distinct feeling that he may have to work a little harder to rate that highly with her. She was no fool. And maybe, if he were honest with himself, he was more of a fool than he wanted to admit.

As he walked back to the cabin, he thought of how the little dog overcame his fear. He wished a piece of cheese would take away all his insecurities. But it wasn't going to be that easy.

Lynne E. Scott

Chapter Fourteen–Trust the Master

With the new training session started, dogs were unruly and owners were nervous. The young boxer lunged at the poodle. The older Golden Retriever sat nicely by its owner's side but whined continuously. Lauren's dog, Scout, stood by her side with his eyes trained on her next move.

"Before a dog can learn the house rules, it must learn to trust the master. I know, I know, it's not politically correct to refer to ourselves as 'masters.' I suppose I should say 'pet partner' or the barely tolerated 'dog owner.' But get over it. To clarify the concept of obedience, I'm using 'master.' It would help for you to look at yourselves as the one in control, rather than the other way around. Training is for the dog's well-being and safety. It is how we communicate with our dogs. Dogs don't understand that they shouldn't chase cars. They don't understand that people frown upon chewing of expensive shoes and furniture. A dog that doesn't have proper training often makes bad decisions."

"Sort of like my kids when they were little?" the boxer owner asked.

Lauren nodded, "Just like that."

*

Giving up on sleep, Michael finally gave in to the temptation he resisted for so long. In one quick, decisive move, he opened the small closet of the cabin, drug out the cardboard box, and rifled through it.

Most of the paperwork were mundane manuals for appliances and so forth. One file was tabbed with "Letter of Recommendation." Michael opened and glanced it over, expecting it to be former letters for Tyler. Instead, he found Tyler's recommendation for Lauren. The top of it read, "For Lauren, from your devoted, yet honest, husband. You thought I was kidding didn't you? Sorry, but let's face some facts about you. The next man needs to know what he's getting into."

Michael paused. He remembered Lauren saying that she and Tyler teased each other often. It was clear from her behavior that she was straightforward about the hard truths of life. But for them to discuss the reality of Lauren having another husband . . . how did Tyler manage that reality? It was beyond Michael's comprehension. He read it over, smiling at some of Tyler's comments.

"Lauren makes a good cup of coffee. Unfortunately, she's not much of a cook. If you like hot sauce, you'll do just fine."

"She is profoundly stubborn and hard-nosed, not unlike her little cattle dog. However, her tenacity is impressive, if not frustrating."

"Lauren will not nag you for your affection, but she'll inspire you to give it freely. She's worth sticking around for, but I, unfortunately, did not have that choice."

Michael set the paper down on his lap, fighting a lump in his throat.

There were only a couple people he knew whose character he admired. At one time, he worked on a film with an older actor whose integrity was unmatched. While most of the time his brother irritated him, if he were faced with serious obstacles in his life he probably could face them. Michael wondered how he would handle a death sentence. It likely wouldn't be with a sense of humor and who knows to what he'd turn to avoid facing it.

His thoughts were interrupted by a knock on the door. He hoped Franny Bottoms wasn't on the other side with one of her unnerving housedresses and casseroles.

He was pleasantly surprised to open the door to Lauren.

She looked radiant as she stood on the front porch, "I thought I should show you my appreciation for making that rail. Just saying the words isn't good enough. It was really nice of you."

Michael waved her off, "It's the least I could do after baiting you the way I did. There's no excuse for it. I'm so sorry."

Lauren sighed, "Let's put it behind us."

"I have no explanation. It was thoughtless and flippant," he paused and looked at her seriously, "You deserve more respect than that."

Lauren frowned, then rolled her eyes, "Oh, please. Don't you go giving me 'The Look.' I can't take it coming from you."

"What's 'The Look'?"

"It is the expression of pity people paste on their faces when they don't know what to say, but want to acknowledge your tragedy, but it comes off as superficial indulgence." Lauren said. "Like this." She twisted her face into a pathetic look of pity and batted her eyes with a head shake. "It's also known, as the 'too bad you failed' look."

Michael nodded, "Oh, that look. Yeah, I know that look. I hate it."

Lauren pulled another expression, "The 'I hope it's not catching' look."

"The 'you're a has-been but I can't politely run away from you' look," Michael said.

"Yes, I see you do understand," Lauren smiled. "Or the 'I would talk to you but you might start crying and I don't want things to be awkward' look."

Michael leaned toward her, "For me, it's the 'you should be crying as I just read your latest movie reviews' look."

They laughed, and suddenly Michael felt a hint of what dealing with reality may feel like after all.

Lauren looked past him in the doorway, "You don't have to, but shouldn't you be inviting me in?"

Michael nearly blushed, "Sorry. I guess I don't have many social graces. Besides, it's your cabin, you can come in whenever you want."

Lauren looked at him like he had two heads, "Right. Because

I'm just going to barge in on you anytime. From the little I know of you, you like your privacy as much as I do. But you're kind to say so." She stepped into the small area and looked around, "It's been a long time since I've been in here."

The file box was sitting on the table, along with the open folder with the letter. Panic rose within him. Lauren's kind tone was about to disappear if she caught him looking through Tyler's personal effects. How could he be so stupid?

Lauren walked slowly toward the kitchen, pausing to look in the open closet.

Michael quickly pushed Lauren into the closet and closed the door.

"Hey! What are you doing?"

He only had two seconds, and he leaped for the folder and stuck it between the sofa cushions and put the box behind the couch. He could hear her fumbling for the door knob.

Michael pounced back to the door and opened it, feigning a playful look on his face, "You know what they say about pay-backs right?"

Lauren stood in the closet with her arms crossed, examining his face, "I hate to say it but I'm starting to understand those bad movie reviews. That is some terrible acting. What is up with you?"

He shook his head and threw his hands up, "You know, come to think of it, my blood sugar is dropping because I haven't eaten anything today."

Lauren lowered her arms and walked toward the door. "Good, I was going to invite you to go to breakfast with me. But try to act normal."

*

Lauren's mixed feelings about going to the diner were outweighed by two things: her hunger and her interest in Michael. It was going to be brutal dealing with the locals, but strangely, she felt up for it today.

As Michael parked his car, Lauren warned him that they would be stared at by everyone. It had little to do with his celebrity but everything about him being a stranger. And to add to the interest, he was a stranger–a male–with Lauren. Soon everyone would be talking.

Michael listened then gave Lauren a dazzling smile, "I'm up for it if you are."

Lauren shrugged back, "What have I got to lose?"

True to her word, the conversation stopped as soon as Lauren and Michael entered the tiny diner. The table where the local farmers gathered turned to gape.

Lauren muttered to Michael, "Maybe this wasn't such a good idea after all."

Just as quickly as the conversation stopped, it restarted with friendly greetings, welcoming Lauren back, with assurances it was good to see her. Lauren's heart warmed. Why had she resisted coming here? After all, each time she was here with Tyler, the farmers were kind and joked with them. Or joked with Tyler anyway. Most of the time she was too tired to join them.

Lauren thanked them, but selected a booth as far from the group as she could, which wasn't very far in such a small room. She slipped into the booth and Michael sat, falling into one of the many holes in the cushions. Lauren grinned as she watched the surprise and discomfort on his face. He bounced around until he found a sturdier spot.

She watched as he surveyed the interior of the diner which consisted of mismatched furniture and exposed wiring hanging from the ceiling. He gave her a look and said, "My tetanus shot isn't up to date. Are you sure it's safe to eat here?"

Lauren raised an eyebrow, "Is that fear I smell?"

"More like an imminent grease fire." Michael looked around, "No menus?"

Lauren gestured toward the wall and Michael noticed a paper plate stuck to the wall with duct tape. "Two eggs, hash browns, toast, no bacon $2.99."

He turned and faced Lauren, "That's it?"

"It's really good."

"What if I want bacon?"

"Don't mess with the system, Michael," Lauren deadpanned, "We don't want your crazy city notions around here, got it?"

"Ahem."

Michael and Lauren noticed Raylene standing behind the counter, her hands on her hips, staring at them.

Michael whispered, "Isn't she the grocery store clerk?"

"Yes, she's sort of omnipresent, but don't use that word around her or you'll confuse her," Lauren whispered back.

"You guys gonna order or what?" Raylene demanded as she marched toward them. "We don't tolerate no sitters around here."

Lauren put her hands up, "We're not sitters, we're eaters."

"Then what do you want, Professor?" Raylene asked Michael.

Lauren shook her head at him, hoping he wouldn't correct her. Fortunately, he took her cue.

"Do you have a no sausage special?" Michael asked, with a straight face.

If Lauren had a menu, she would have buried her face in it to keep from laughing. Instead, she pinched her nose and looked at the table.

Raylene frowned, "We don't do special orders."

"Oh, then I will have the no bacon special. Or not have it."

Raylene turned her head toward Lauren, who looked up, struggling to keep a stoic look. But she wasn't fast enough for Raylene, who gestured at her impatiently. "You want your usual?"

Lauren cleared her throat, "That would be great."

As she walked away, Lauren pinched her nose again.

"Why do you keep doing that?" Michael asked.

"It's to keep from laughing. It works to keep from crying, so I thought maybe it would work for laughing."

"Did it?"

"Not really, but my nose really hurts now."

Michael leaned forward after making sure Raylene was a safe distance away, "She has no name tag, no uniform."

Lauren leaned forward conspiratorially with him, "And most important, no sense of humor."

Michael grinned at her. Lauren felt her face flush ever so much. She hoped he would think it was the heat, which swirled around them as the fan oscillated.

"You must be a regular."

Lauren cast her eyes down, "I used to be."

"Ah, got it," Michael nodded, and thankfully changed the subject, "So tell me, Dog Lady, what's it like to have a kennel?"

Lauren shrugged, "We started it out of necessity. It wasn't really part of my life plan, but so far none of it has been. However, it's better than the two Ps."

Michael waited for her explanation.

"People and pantyhose," Lauren said. "No co-workers and no uncomfortable clothing."

"You know pantyhose are out of style, don't you?"

Lauren frowned, "I'm not sure if I'm more disturbed to hear this or that you know it." She looked around. "Huh, I wish there were memos on such things."

"There are these things called fashion magazines," Michael said.

"Right, because as you can tell, fashion is really important to me," Lauren snorted as she pointed to her T-shirt which had a small tear in the shoulder.

Michael shook his head, but Lauren could tell he wasn't as horrified as he acted.

"I really need some coffee. Is customer service this bad?"

Lauren indicated the coffee station that sat near a wooden pillar in the center of the diner. "It's self-serve."

Michael looked back at her, "This place is so glamorous."

As he got up, she shot back, "We read about it in a fashion magazine."

He smirked as he looked back at her, "This better not be one of your set-ups."

Lauren feigned a look of innocence and shrugged.

Michael poured two mugs of coffee. As he walked back to the table, he noticed the farmers watching him. "Do they want my autograph?"

"They want coffee," Lauren said as she accepted her cup. "When one person gets up, it's customary to top off everyone else's cup too."

Michael considered this as he set down his mug, "That's small town charm."

"It also may be profound laziness."

Lauren thoroughly enjoyed the sight of Michael Quinlan picking up the pot of coffee and pouring coffee for the farmers at the table.

A very thin farmer thanked Michael and asked, "Who're you?"

Before Michael could answer, another man answered, "He's that new guy helping out Jim for the summer theater stuff."

The first man looked at Michael, "I sure wish they'd stick with satire. I don't think farce is good humor."

Again, the other man answered, "To do satire right, you really need to love what you're satirizing." He looked at Michael, "Ain't that right?"

"Sure, yes," Michael said. The men continued their debate, but didn't include Michael so he walked away to return the coffee pot.

"Son, could you bring me a couple packets of Splenda?" the thin farmer asked.

"And some non-dairy creamer," the other man ordered.

Lauren put her hand over her mouth to hide her laugh when Michael gave her a look of complete mystification. After he finished helping the farmers, then pouring two cups of coffee for a couple that seated themselves nearby, he returned to Lauren.

"My coffee is probably cold by now," he said as he sat uncomfortably on the bumpy cushions.

"I can see the headline now, "Michael Quinlan leaves Miss California for Mr. Coffee."

"You're really not very funny, you know that?" Michael sighed as he sipped his drink. "Maybe waiting tables is my true calling."

"You're thinking of quitting?" Lauren was genuinely surprised.

"I've got the two Ps working against me–Privacy and Parts." Michael responded to Lauren's frown, "Parts meaning parts in movies, roles, you know. The parts I'm offered these days are pathetic."

"You've been at it a long time," Lauren consoled.

"Those donuts have a longer shelf life than my career," Michael nodded toward the case by the cash register that held a few pastries.

"You should help Jim. It would be good for you."

"I don't have much to offer college students. It's a different world."

Lauren found herself repeating words she'd heard, "You may decide that now, but you may un-decide it later."

Michael looked at her the same way she looked at Alice when she heard the phrase. He thought a moment and said, "Somehow that makes sense."

Their meals arrived, and Lauren's plate was twice as full as Michael's. Raylene said nothing as she served them and set down silverware before walking away.

"That's an impressive amount of food," Michael said.

"I told you I was hungry."

Michael reached for the silverware but Lauren grabbed his hand. She took both sets and sprayed them with sanitizing solution she pulled from her bag. She handed his back.

"Now it smells like vanilla," Michael complained.

"You'll thank me later."

They both began eating. "This is surprisingly good," Michael said, his mouth half full.

"I wouldn't be a regular if it was awful," Lauren answered.

Michael shrugged, "It's not like you have options."

"There are always options." Lauren stated, "If you left acting, it wouldn't be the end of the world. I mean, you've got plenty of life in front of you."

Michael paused, "One might say the same thing to you." When she ignored him, he added, "What do you do around here for fun?"

Lauren snorted, "I'm not exactly scrapbooking my memories."

She looked up and saw the startled look on Michael's face, "I'm sorry, maybe that was too flippant. But really, someone once invited me to a scrapbook party and it was the worst thing in the world for me. My whole peer group made their pages with pictures of their children, fabulous vacations, marathons the couple ran together. What was I supposed to do?"

Michael grimaced, "So what did you do?"

"I made a montage of cat pictures. I figured I might as well get a jump on the crazy cat lady title."

Michael laughed, "You can't be the crazy cat lady and the dog lady at the same time."

"I don't see why not," Lauren said.

After they finished their meals, Lauren watched as Michael paid Raylene and gave her a hefty tip. Her sour attitude quickly changed. Before they got out the door, a mother with her young daughter entered. The daughter raced over to Lauren and hugged her legs.

Lauren kneeled down to hug her properly, "Jackie! I've missed you!"

"I miss you too. Can we do 'Ten Little Monkeys?' " Jackie asked.

Lauren looked up at Jackie's mom, and shook her head, "Not here, Jackie."

"Then let's do 'Two Little Blackbirds!' "

Before Lauren could stop her the little girl put her fists out with one finger raised on each hand, "Two little blackbirds sitting on a hill. One named Jack. One named Jill."

The little girl stopped, waiting for Lauren to join. She did, and put her hands out the same way, facing Jackie. Together they chanted, "Fly away Jack!" One hand went on their shoulder, "Fly away Jill!" The other hand went to the other shoulder. "Come back Jack!" They brought the hand back. "Come back Jill!" Both hands were back, the two little fingers side by side.

Lauren paused to look at the little fingers, feeling suddenly emotional. Jackie clapped her hands and jumped up and down.

"That's enough, Jackie." Her mother said sternly. Jackie danced away and chanted the ditty over and over.

Lauren stood slowly, "Hi, Carly."

Carly's voice was very shallow, "How are you?"

Lauren grimaced. Carly was giving her 'the Look.' Michael walked over to her side. Lauren managed a small, "Okay."

"Sorry I haven't called. You know, we've just been so busy." Carly gushed.

Lauren waited, watching Carly fidget, "Sure. I understand completely."

When Lauren walked into the parking lot, she hardly remembered she was with Michael. Lost in her thoughts, she looked for her own pickup truck. Finally realizing where she was, she followed Michael to his car, slamming the door as she got in next to Michael.

"Ever notice how some friends drop you when you're not useful or convenient anymore?"

Before Michael turned the key in the ignition, he paused and smiled at Lauren with what looked to be genuine understanding, "Welcome to my world."

Chapter Fifteen—A Tired Dog is a Good Dog

The next day, Lauren woke up unusually early. Her energy level was off the chart and she whistled airily, which was out of the ordinary. Maybe it was that old movie she saw that inspired her to just put her lips together and blow. She reminded herself not to think about kissing.

Since spending time with Michael yesterday, her brain seemed to be popping in a different way. Her heart sure was, not that she wanted to think too hard about that. By six thirty in the morning, the dogs were out, fed, and walked, her dishes were done, and breakfast was over.

Guinness kept poking her with his nose and staring at her. After she read the paper, she looked at her list of things to do. For too long she ignored the little tasks she hated. Part of it simply was she didn't know how to do some of them.

Suddenly, Guinness tore past her, chasing his favorite cat, Parsnip, who often wrestled with the giant dog. "Guinness, leave it! Let's go for a walk."

Guinness bounded into the room, followed by Scout, and soon they were on the road. She hated it when she forgot her most basic advice for unruly dogs. "Tire them out."

Misbehavior often occurred because the dog had too much physical energy, as well as not being mentally stimulated.

Lauren noticed Guinness' tail was extra plumy today. She had not seen him so alert since Tyler died. While always an obedient dog, he often seemed to respond begrudgingly to her. Today he was alert and interested in the world. The walk would do them all good. There was too much to do once she returned. She had to stop putting things off and she'd definitely feel better when progress was made.

As Lauren walked with the dogs, she remembered how early in their marriage before either of them knew anything about the disease that would consume both of their lives, Lauren and Tyler repaired part of the deck on their back porch. It didn't take long for Lauren to realize that hammering didn't come naturally. The first clue was Tyler laughing and shaking his head in disbelief at her ineptitude. The second was her bruised finger. Then there was the time they painted their bedroom when they first moved into their home. Same effect–Tyler laughing and a butter-yellow hand and forearm on Lauren.

No wonder she dreaded home repairs. When she returned, she put the leashes away and decided to attack the easiest task– replacing a light bulb in the kitchen fixture. She felt confident of her abilities in this arena.

As she got out the creaky step stool, she smiled at the sounds of Guinness wrestling with Parsnip in the living room. That walk seemed to provide Guinness with more energy instead of wearing him out. Scout barked his encouragement at the commotion. As she replaced the lamp over the working bulb, Guinness peeled into the kitchen, pursued by the cat.

When they made a lap around the island in the kitchen, the step stool, with Lauren upon it, was knocked over.

Lying on her back, Lauren suffered further indignity when the cat raced right over her chest, still pursuing Guinness back into the living room. Scout proceeded to lick her face.

"So much for pets sensing their owner's pain," Lauren moaned as she sat up. At least she didn't hit her head. However, her ankle was tangled with the step stool and island. "Great," Lauren said, feeling the pain throb.

She carefully stood and hobbled to the freezer. As she sat at the dining room table with an ice pack on her foot, she wondered what to do next. Alice was at an all-day beekeeping seminar. Jim was at the theater. Tish was working. Somehow she couldn't imagine Michael scooping dog poop. Not that he would agree. Not that she planned to ask.

When it was time to let the dogs out, she grit her teeth and carefully made her way to the kennel. It wasn't the first time she worked wounded. Dogs had knocked her over a few times before, banging up her arm as she fell. An over eager dog jumped on the cage gate just as Lauren opened it, giving her a black eye. Then there was the time she had the flu. However, an ankle was different, and this hurt with every step she took.

As one dog sprinted out of its cage, sure enough, it jumped on her, causing her to lose her footing. The dog walked out of the open back door into the fenced in area while Lauren grabbed her ankle.

"Lauren!"

She looked up to see Michael enter from the front door. As he kneeled by her, inspecting her ankle, she burst into tears. Then she was mad. This was so embarrassing.

"What happened?" he asked, helping her back on her feet.

Fortunately her tears dried quickly, telling the story with humor instead.

"Why didn't you call me?"

"Trust me, this is one role you don't want to play."

The look he gave her melted her heart. Somehow he managed to look tender without making her feel like a charity case. Michael asked her what needed done and she told him, watching from a chair that he retrieved from her office.

The dogs jumped in excitement when they saw a new person. "They always do that," Lauren told him as Michael quickly was covered in paw prints.

He laughed as he coaxed a schnauzer into its kennel run, the dog jumping up and licking his hands when he tried to direct him. "I'm beginning to understand why you do this."

"It can be a lot of fun," Lauren admitted. It was true, though often she forgot about it when it was busy.

Finally the work was done and Michael steadied Lauren as she hobbled out of the kennel. On the front stoop, she stepped down too hard and let out a small cry.

"Wimp," Michael said, scooping her into his arms and carrying her toward the house.

For the first time in years, Lauren was speechless. She giggled like a schoolgirl and as soon as she did, she wanted to die. It was completely involuntary. He playfully jostled her and she kept giggling.

Settling her on the couch and bringing the ice pack to her, Michael righted the toppled step stool. "It's none of my business, but don't you have neighbors who can do this for you?"

"I should be able to change my own lightbulbs," Lauren said. "Alice and Jim can't do all my chores."

"Yes, but I've noticed there's a lot to be done around here."

Lauren grimaced as she adjusted the ice pack, "You might be surprised how many women won't let their husbands help me. Apparently they think widows are sex fiends who will hit on their husbands."

Michael looked her over, causing her to blush, "What about a handyman?"

"After a couple hit on me, I decided against it."

Michael sat by her, "You're going to need some help. I promise not to hit on you if you'll find me one of those sex fiend widows."

Lauren laughed, "There must be plenty. But isn't this when you start helping Jim with rehearsals?"

Michael nodded, "Classic plays, amateur actors, and a dozen dogs to feed. My life hasn't been this interesting in a long time."

"Yeah, things are really working out for you, aren't they?"

Lauren teased. That strange feeling of energy coursing through her veins drove out the pain in her ankle. It hit her like a ton of bricks when she realized it was attraction.

*

After a shower to remove the dog slobber, Michael drove to the college. While he mocked his "full life" comment to Lauren, he quietly admitted that life was indeed stimulating. Lauren was a major component in this. She wasn't the classic beauty or even manufactured beauty he saw in his world, but she drew his interest, and not just physically.

However, helping with the kennel cut into his time familiarizing himself with *She Stoops to Conquer*. Normally, research was an important part of his preparation. He sat in the front row of the theater, engrossed in the script as Jim stood watching the rehearsal. The college students looked so young.

Monty played the part of the lead, Marlow, while his on-again, off-again girlfriend, Pam, was his love interest, Miss Hardcastle.

Monty impressed Michael, as he followed along with the part of Marlow, "I protest, child you use me extremely ill. If you keep me at this distance, how is it possible you and I can ever be acquainted?"

Pam, on the other hand, was hasty with her lines of Miss Hardcastle, "And who wants to be acquainted with you? I want no such acquaintance, not I. I'm sure you did not treat–"

Pam tossed her script across the stage, "This is ridiculous. Why doesn't Miss Hardcastle just tell Marlow to get lost?"

Monty joined her, "Yeah, and he could have just told Miss Hardcastle she was hot and save a lot of words."

"Part of the reason we're studying a play written one hundred years ago is to appreciate the use of words. It's not necessarily the amount we're concerned with. Consider the approach as well as the word choice. It's a dance." Jim said calmly.

"Why are we doing such old stuff anyway?" Monty asked.

Michael found himself feeling less charitable than Jim. No wonder Jim worked with college students. Michael had no patience for their attitude. Didn't these kids realize the beauty of the writing? Was texting all they thought of? He realized he was thinking like an old timer. Next thing he knew, he'd utter, "back in my day."

Yet he couldn't sit there without saying anything. Lauren must be wearing off on him. He approached the stage, "Jim's right. Part of what you're learning is what makes for a classic piece of literature. If you want to act as a professional, you need to know what quality is and what is pandering to the audience."

Michael stopped, wondering if anyone would accuse him of choosing less than quality parts, which was true. He might as well come clean, "I've taken roles that weren't my favorites in films I think now were mostly unwatchable. However, that is a different part of your education. Right now, we're talking about literature. These plays are still relevant. They've stood the test of time."

Monty snorted, "So has *Wheel of Fortune*. Does that mean it's a classic?"

"What do you know? You only watched it when that Kelly was there. Man, you drooled over her." Pam shook her head in disgust.

Monty shrugged his shoulders, "She was hot. Besides, have you read her blog? It's amazing."

Part of Michael wanted to punch Monty in the nose. It likely had more to do with his shallowness than wanting to defend Kelly's honor, since she had little. When he was their age, was he that much different? Part of him was, but maybe now honorable wasn't his strongest character trait.

Clearly they were way off track. Michael, bewildered at the turn of the conversation, struggled to remain professional.

"Each of you was given a part that you didn't necessarily choose. Honestly, that may happen to you often, so make the most of what you're given. If you want to be considered a professional, you make it look easy."

After rehearsal was over, Michael felt exhausted. It wasn't the play, it was the cast. He had no idea how Jim didn't blow a gasket, but he kept his cool. Indeed, he was a professional because he made it look easy. Maybe later they could talk it out over a beer. That sure sounded good to him right now.

Pam approached him as most of the cast filed out, "Mickey? I'd love to have you read lines with me." She batted her eyes at him and stood too close, "You know, put me through my paces?" she whispered the last part breathily, her lips apart as she looked at his.

Michael stepped back, disturbed by her forwardness. Maybe

she did have what it took to be a professional actress after all. "No offense, Pam, but how old are you?"

Undeterred, Pam took another step closer. She was inches from his face, "Your age doesn't bother me. Why should mine bother you?"

Ick. Michael was thankful when a testy Monty took Pam by the arm.

Monty scowled at Michael, "Come on, Pam. Let's go."

Pam shot one more hopeful look at Michael as she left with Monty. Michael could still hear them arguing. Particularly Monty's accusation that he was old enough to be Pam's father. That was going a bit too far. Then Michael did the math and realized it was true. That was disturbing to him. However, he found Pam's behavior even more disturbing. So this is what it looks like from the other side. He knew for certain this was Kelly's normal behavior, only probably even more aggressive. It was decidedly unattractive.

That evening, he found himself pouring over the play, examining the passages thoroughly. The banter was light, but spoke volumes. With so many sequels and remakes of old movies, he wondered if anyone might be working on an updated version of it. Or maybe even *Our Town*. He missed movies that were actually about something.

He called Tom to ask him to make inquiries for him.

"I'll do some checking for you. I like where you're going with this, Mick." Tom's tone pleased Michael.

"It's the first time I've been excited about a potential project in a long time. These stories have so much heart."

"Speaking of heart, have you kept up with Kelly's antics?"

Michael realized thoughts of Kelly had disappeared until Monty brought her up, "She's off my radar."

"She's getting some press as a popular blogger. She somehow gets an inside track on just about everything. She must know people."

"She sure isn't getting it from me," Michael said. "I smell a rat."

"Are you sure it's a rat? Maybe you just stepped in something over at the kennel," Tom teased. "I heard you've been helping Lauren."

"You seem to have an inside lead on news too, Tom."

"Anyway, just wanted to give you an update that Kelly's making progress in her quest to become a player out here," Tom said.

After Michael hung up, he thought of what Tom said. Honestly, he found the kennel work sort of entertaining. Most of the dogs were friendly and the owners were usually in a good mood when they came back from their vacations. Did he even care about Kelly's antics? It seemed so far away now. So inconsequential. If he compared that to the lack of integrity in so many with whom he'd worked over the course of his career, it might be hard to decide if a kennel was full of more crap than Hollywood.

Chapter Sixteen–Praise Their Progress

Lauren's ankle was better, and she was back to her daily work. However, training classes still required her to use a chair as she talked with the dog owners. She was pleased to see that Michael continued to help with Goliath. In some ways, the dog was making even more progress with Michael. Perhaps it was his long legs that caused the little dog to work even harder to keep up with him.

This was no time to consider Michael's legs or any other of his body parts. She'd seen his arm muscles once and she wasn't sure what she'd do if she pondered his physique too much. Probably pass out. That would look bad in front of a room full of dogs. Now, where was she anyway?

"You've all been doing well with your homework since your dogs are definitely listening to you more. Now we'll move on to something a little different."

The owners followed Lauren over to another part of the training area that contained the obstacle course. There were a few small jumps, a tunnel, a large ramp, and other obstacles. Lauren glanced at Michael in time to see him looking at her. She felt herself blush. Darn it. This was something she did since she was young, and it was awful. Maybe when she was a little older she could blame hot flashes.

"Probably most of you are looking at this and wondering what it has to do with your dog's obedience. A show of hands–how many of you plan to train your dog to do obedience competitions?"

Not one raised a hand.

Lauren nodded, "Then why bother learning the obstacle course? For one thing, this is an opportunity for you to interact in a different way with your dog. Believe it or not, this mental stimulation is fun for a dog. You build a bond with your dog when they learn to listen to you. Going up a ramp gives them a sense of accomplishment."

Guinness ran up the ramp and down the other side, then jumped on a raised platform where he sat, watching Lauren for her next cue.

"When we adopted Guinness, he was afraid and hid behind a chair the best way a one hundred pound black dog could hide. While he did well with simple obedience commands, it wasn't until we started the obstacle course that he changed. Being able to accomplish something difficult is better than avoiding the discomfort and fear."

As the owners formed a line to try the different challenges, Lauren added, "Another good thing about obstacles is it gives you the chance to compliment your dog on doing something the right way. With the mistakes they may be making with the other commands, if you end on a positive note, they enjoy training much more. Always be sure to catch them doing something right, then give them a treat."

*

Michael rifled through Tyler's tool box, feeling as if this was even more intrusive than the box of personal effects in the cabin. Michael's dad took him along to do odd jobs for friends when he wasn't fixing up their own Victorian home. He always said you could tell a lot about a man by how they cared for their tools, not just what was in the tool box. From the looks of things, Tyler knew what he was doing in both scope and maintenance of tools.

Once he finished patching a hole in the lean-to from Lauren's shot gun, he began work on her back screen door. Lauren came out to water the lush garden of plants. It was practically a forest.

"Looks like an Italian garden back here," Michael commented.

"Thanks. That was the look I was going for, since we never made it to Italy." Lauren set the watering can down and watched Michael work.

The back of his neck warmed under her scrutiny. It may have been the morning sun, but he could practically feel her gaze. Not knowing what else to say, he tried for small talk, "I'm surprised by how many tools you have."

"I'm surprised you know how to use them," Lauren shot back. "Think you can take care of my mailbox?"

"What happened to it? It looks like someone hit it with a baseball bat."

"It was hit by a baseball bat. That is the perverse summer

game for some. But in the winter, my mailbox gets hit by the snowplow at least twice. That's why there's no mailbox for the cabin. No point having both replaced." Lauren grinned, "It's all very exciting."

Michael smiled in appreciation at her wit, "I can't wait to tell my agent, Tom, I repaired a gunshot in a barn."

"If you really want to brag, I could make more." Lauren gave out a small screech as one of her cats sprinted across the porch toward the door, a mouse in its mouth. Michael dropped the tool and stood, flattening himself against the door.

"No!" Lauren leapt to the entrance to block the cat, "Get back! Outside toys stay outside!"

The cat stood staring at Lauren. Two more cats joined it, investigating the first one's treasure. This caused the first one to growl and dart away.

Lauren sighed. Michael went back to work, "I take it mice in the house has happened before?"

"More than I'd like to admit."

"No wonder this is a priority," Michael said, sealing the last hole. "That should do it."

Lauren laughed ruefully, "Perfect. Thanks. You have no idea how awful it is during grasshopper season."

Michael stood and looked at her, trying to see if she was serious.

"I once came home from the grocery store and as I was putting the bags down, a grasshopper with one back leg stared at me, just out of reach of its cat audience."

"It sounds strangely like awards season in Hollywood." Michael sat on the patio chair as Lauren brought them out coffee from the kitchen. Guinness brought Michael a tennis ball, which he dropped at his feet, waiting for Michael to throw it.

As Michael picked it up, Lauren warned, "You may regret that. Once you start with him, he'll expect you to continue for an hour or two."

"Guinness and I go way back," Michael said, throwing the ball in an impressive arc.

"Really? He's been so timid without Tyler around," Lauren murmured.

"He comes over for a visit almost every day." Michael watched as a large black and white cat stretched itself out on the table. "Anyone ever try to do an intervention with you on the number of cats you have?"

Lauren snorted, "You sound like-" She stopped and looked down, "Each one has been dumped off here. The shelter won't take any more cats since they've declared themselves 'no kill.' I give them a chance."

Michael leaned back, and looked out at the cornfield that ran behind Lauren's home. "The corn makes for a nice privacy fence for your pond. Do you swim much?"

"As much as I can," Lauren smiled.

"Really? How have I missed seeing you in your bathing

suit?" Michael teased.

Lauren raised her mug to take a sip, "I'm very discreet."

He grinned at her, closing his eyes for a moment. It was so blissfully quiet here. His whole body was relaxed, a wonderful change from needing weekly massages to undo the stress knots he carried most of the time. He couldn't believe he used to think less of people who lived in the country, as if they weren't smart enough to earn a place in the excitement of the city. Sipping coffee, listening to a cat purr, feeling the warmth of Lauren by his side. He couldn't recall a time he felt so . . . so what? He thought a minute longer. Content. He felt content. He didn't even feel like he needed to make conversation. The quiet was companionable.

He glanced over at Lauren, who looked as relaxed as he did, with her feet up, one hand sipping from her mug, the other absently rubbing the cat's ears.

"These mugs are really cool," Michael commented, not comfortable with extended silence.

Lauren looked at hers, "Alice made them."

"Alice?" Michael sat up and looked at her. She must be kidding about this. "Alice, Jim's wife, made these?"

"Redbeans herself," Lauren smiled. "She's got a potter's wheel, kiln, and all that stuff at her house."

Michael's brows crinkled. It was as if Lauren read his mind when she said, "You think people in the country are incapable of fine arts? There's a little shop in town that sells her work, along with the works of other local artists."

"I never thought of myself as a snob, but I guess I have been," Michael said, putting his feet back up. "I guess I figured being this isolated, not much culture happened. That was an ignorant theory."

Lauren stood and stretched, "Glad you're seeing the 'error of your ways.' Now go tell everyone we're not a bunch of rubes. I thought the same thing when I moved here. And I'm guilty of errant snobbery here and there still."

"The velvet ropes keep me with my own kind," Michael mused. "I don't miss them. You can't move freely within them."

"You know what you need?" Lauren grinned, "Hard work."

For the next week, Michael found himself happily busy. He repaired some bent fence wire in the kennel, with Guinness by his side until Lauren ordered him away. She helped him steady a wooden fence post that bent at a perilous angle by her propane tank. He even helped fill a trench made by a kennel client's tires in the lawn. Lauren scattered grass seed over the dirt as he carefully packed it over the area.

"We make a pretty good team, huh?" Michael said without thinking.

Lauren froze as a handful of seed fell short of its target. Michael read the expression on her face as simple fear. How stupid could he be? "Maybe we could start our own handyman company," he tried.

She stood and looked at him, then at the ground. He thought for a minute she might burst into tears.

A kennel client drove past them and up to the door, a giant St. Bernard panting out the open window. When Lauren went over to meet them, he knew he wasn't the only one to feel relieved.

As Michael picked up the bag of grass seed and finished spreading it over the dirt, he occasionally glanced over to watch Lauren interact with the dog owners.

It was a picture of chaos. The motor of the vehicle continued to run. The dog was trying to crawl out the window as four children screeched with delight. The dad sprang out of the driver's side, leaving the door open. The dog's head was awkwardly caught in the window, which the man tried to push back in the car. Then the man sprinted to the trunk, took out a huge pail of dog food and placed it at Lauren's feet. By this time, the dog had crawled from the back seat and out the driver's door, wandering around without a leash.

The giant dog lumbered up to Lauren, wagging its tail. Michael couldn't hear the question Lauren yelled to the owner above the commotion of the children's squeals and the dog's woofs. Apparently the man didn't either as he hopped back into the car, shut the door, and put it into gear making a wide arc over the grass and out the driveway.

Michael watched as the car swerved within three feet of where he stood, and crossed the fresh dirt, forcing the seed into the ground. The man waved and laughed, like it was a very funny joke. The children did the same, and one yelled, "We're going to Disney World!"

At the same time, the dog realized his family was leaving. It turned from Lauren to pursue the car as it sped away. Michael noticed just in time to see Lauren leap on top of the dog, grabbing the back half in her arms. The dog continued to move and she slid to the ground.

"A little help!" she yelled.

Michael dropped the seed bag and raced to Lauren, securing the front end of the dog. Still, the massive beast whined and pressed forward down the driveway. Now Michael slipped and held the dog by the neck.

"There's no collar!" Michael yelled.

"Don't let go, whatever you do!" Lauren yelled. "I've got a slip leash in the office." She sprinted for the leash.

Suddenly forgetting all about its owner, the dog noticed Michael. At this point, Michael was just about eye to eye with it. The dog stopped panting and gave him a long look.

"Please don't eat me," Michael muttered, loosening his grip just a tiny bit. He may have to bolt for the office in a second too.

The dog opened its mouth and lunged for Michael, licking his face with a vengeance. There was no winning. "Stop!" Michael said, to no effect.

The next thing Michael heard was Lauren's laughter. She appeared over him, looped a leash quickly and slipped it over the dog's enormous head, interrupting the licking, but only for a moment.

"Yuck! Get it away from me!" Michael, with his hands finally free, covered his face.

Lauren pulled on the leash and called the dog. Immediately the dog followed Lauren. As they disappeared through the kennel door, Michael got up and dusted himself off. He was due at the theater for rehearsal in a half hour. He had some changing to do.

Chapter Seventeen–It's Worth Staying

"Jim and Alice were over last night," Lauren said as she helped Michael replace a blade on her ceiling fan. "Jim said the students really enjoy your help at the rehearsals. Apparently they hang on your every word."

Michael gave her a funny look, "That might be overstating it."

Lauren was afraid to ask what she really wanted to know, "Are you enjoying it?"

"Yeah, but I figured out last night that part of what I'm enjoying is when I read lines or demonstrate form," Michael shrugged. "It reminded me of the joy of performing."

Lauren was thankful he couldn't see her look of disappointment. It was impossible to hide it. Ever since she caught a glimpse of him chopping wood behind the barn the other day, sleep wasn't easy to come by.

"Did I tell you Franny Bottoms stopped over yesterday afternoon when I came back from here?" Michael asked, stepping down from the ladder.

"More casserole, I suppose."

"Actually she told me Goliath is the very model of good dog behavior." He walked by her, "We have you to thank for that."

When he said 'you,' he tapped her nose with his index finger as he walked by.

"Have you helped him with the next challenge for class?" Lauren tried not to think too hard about his playful contact. However, her heart racing wouldn't let her forget.

"Why does a dog have to stay for seven minutes? Goliath is good for about three minutes, then he goes to look for Franny." Michael made a final adjustment. "I never thought I'd be spending my days playing hide and seek with a tiny dog and an old lady."

"Security. If the dog can't be confident in his owner's command when they are out of the room, then they haven't really learned. Insecurity causes the dog to break and try to find its owner. They need to trust they will be back. After all, they should realize their owners are worth sticking around for, shouldn't they?"

Michael smirked, "Like Franny would ever leave Goliath."

"But Goliath has left Franny to do his own thing, that's why he's in obedience class to begin with."

"Let's pretend you can carry on a conversation that doesn't involve dogs," Michael put the step stool away and jabbed a pouting Lauren as he walked by. "Anyway, I was sore from all that wood chopping the other day and I was moving pretty slowly. Franny made me sit in a chair." He reached in the refrigerator, took a beer and handed one to her before sliding open the patio door.

Lauren followed him, like a pathetic, helpless puppy. "And?"

"She massaged my shoulders." Michael gave her a long look.

Lauren couldn't move. Was she jealous? Horrified? Hard to know. "And how did you feel about that? I mean, I'm thinking it's kind of weird myself."

Michael nodded, "Yes, but she's remarkably skilled." He leaned forward and hunched a shoulder at her expectantly.

"What do you want?" Lauren popped open the beer and ignored him and sat alongside him, looking out over the pond.

"Can't you take a hint?"

"Sure," Lauren took a gulp, "Can't you? I see your hint and raise it by ignoring it."

"Touché."

The crickets began their song as the afternoon slipped into evening. Lauren liked how they spent time together without having to constantly make conversation. It reminded her of the first time she realized that when she was with Tyler in the car, they never listened to the radio. She used to always have the radio on. That's when she realized Tyler was someone worth loving.

She took a long pull of the beer. The implications of this were disturbing. She snuck a look at his long frame, as he stretched his legs out and yawned. Another gulp of beer was in order.

"No wonder you farm folk go to bed early. All this physical work wears me out." He stood up and took her empty beer bottle eyeing it with a wink. "You know I've never slept better than I have out here."

As he walked into the kitchen to get another beer, Lauren muttered, "That makes one of us."

Michael handed her another beer, "Did you say something?"

"Just that a tired dog is a good dog," Lauren said quickly.

"You're really quite a flirt." Michael sat and took a slug of beer. "Franny said something about you being a judge for some fund-raiser?"

"She sure does talk."

Michael nodded, "I imagine you giving your opinion is one of your favorite things. So what is it?"

"Franny Bottoms told you I was the judge but didn't tell you about the event?" Lauren was incredulous. "She's one of the biggest contributors."

"That surprises me. She doesn't look like she has a lot of money."

Lauren rolled her eyes, "Oh no. It's not money." She sighed heavily. "The Dog House Show is the big event of the season around here. Every business in town and many individuals decorate a dog house and enter it into a contest. Franny tends to enter many dog houses."

"Does she win?"

Lauren's expression made it clear that she didn't. "She's not much of a crafter. That doesn't stop her though. Sometimes I think the chicken casseroles are because I'm the judge."

"Right, trying to win you over."

"Or punish me for not picking her."

Michael quipped, "Life sure is complicated around here."

"You should come to the fund-raiser. It's really a lot of fun. Alice and Jim cook a special meal, and there's a pie contest too." Lauren realized she was talking too fast and probably too excitedly. She stopped and sat back, giving Michael an embarrassed look, "Wow, I guess I've really become one of these small town people. You probably find the whole idea ridiculous."

"Not at all," Michael smiled. "It sounds charming in that weird small town way I'm learning. But who knows, maybe I will have a job by then."

Of course. How could she get her hopes up like that? "Right. There's really not much worth sticking around for here besides festivals, town gossip and dog slobber."

"Is that what you're worried about? I'm going to leave all this because it's not worth it?" He placed his hand on her arm. "If I leave, it's because I have my career pressing at me. It's not because anything or anyone is driving me away."

Lauren looked away, "That's not what I meant."

"Listen, I didn't know you when you were married to Tyler. Tyler sounds like a man I would have liked to meet. From what

I know of you right now, you're handling what happened then and what is happening now like it's easy."

She felt like she was going to cry. If he only knew. "Tyler knew what I was capable of."

Michael nodded, "Sure. You've got strength, perseverance."

Lauren gulped, looking out on the pond, listening to the frogs as they began their song. "No. It was more like desperation. Maybe even rage. It just seemed like neither Ty nor I were equipped to handle it as well as we should have. Or at least as well as I should have."

Michael moved closer and said softly, "Lauren, listen to me. I can't pretend to know what you endured. But I will tell you, you're not the only one who grieves losing what they once had. It's not on the same level, but you're looking at a man who knows a lot about desperation."

She turned away from him. "Maybe we both don't measure up to the standards others have set for us."

"I'm starting to admit it," Michael gently pushed against her, "How about you?"

Chapter Eighteen–Choosing to Listen

Lauren cupped his face with both her hands and looked adoringly into his eyes. "You're never too old to learn."

The response was a kiss on the tip of her nose. Lauren patted the mastiff on his head, which was almost at eye level. "He's a beautiful dog, and of course he can come to obedience classes. You don't want a dog this size misbehaving."

The owner paid Lauren the boarding bill, "This breed can be so stubborn. He doesn't seem interested in changing his ways."

"In other words, Tank knows the rules, but resists following them?" Lauren noted the enthusiastic nod. "So we have to figure out how to shift the voice of authority that he will obey. It will require some patience, but we can persuade Tank that obeying is not only worthwhile, but it may be fun."

*

As the two of them drove to the diner, Michael considered how his eating habits had changed since arriving here. Funny how all that work made him so hungry. Suddenly all the hearty food offered at the diner made sense. There was no way he could order sausage gravy and biscuits or a fried tenderloin sandwich with tater tots at his usual haunts. If his friends saw him now, they would look down their noses at him. Certainly that was his attitude until a few short weeks ago.

Michael decided to share his musings with Lauren, who rode with one arm casually out the open window. They got in the habit of taking her pickup to the diner. Somehow his sports car just looked out of place. However, he stipulated that he would drive.

"You mentioned Alice is a vegetarian. Does she ever eat at the diner?"

Lauren laughed, which surprised Michael. Her seriousness of earlier dissipated. "She eats eggs and toast. A true vegan may have a bit of a drive to find a place where they could find something suitable."

Over their dinner, Michael continued to enjoy her lighter mood. He shared stories with her just to keep her laughing. The farmers were at their usual table, and one topped off Michael's coffee for him with a tip of his ball cap.

Lauren's eyes darted to the table as the farmer returned to his friends. Finally she leaned forward, "It appears we are the subject of their conversation today. They keep jabbing each other and pointing in our direction."

"Should we kiss and give them something worthy of discussion?"

The blush that flooded Lauren's cheeks warmed Michael. It was refreshing to see a woman who was still capable of being shocked. "Your red cheeks are flattering. How did you manage to get on stage and act?" Michael asked. "I saw the posters over at the theater. Jim said you weren't bad."

"I wasn't good either." Lauren laughed. "Acting's different, isn't it? For one thing, you're in control of your lines, delivery, character and scenery. Real life is completely unpredictable. You just never know when someone might tease you with an absurd offer."

Michael grinned and leaned forward, "It wasn't that absurd."

Looking down at her food, her cheeks flushed again, "Come on, I'm trying to eat here." She took a bite of eggs.

"Guess you like the diner's all day breakfast option."

"I love breakfast. It makes me feel like I'm on vacation."

Michael considered that. If he wanted to feel like he was on vacation, he went on vacation. "Back to acting, what was your favorite role?"

Lauren sighed, "I don't know. I can't remember the Lauren who was in college."

"How did you get interested in theater?"

Lauren took a bite of toast and shook her head at him.

Michael opened his hands to her, "How is this a trick question? Tell me."

"Fine," Lauren put down her fork, "When I was in high school, there was this up and coming actor, about the same age as me. I thought the movies were charming and that he was very talented."

She looked at him steadily.

It was Michael's turn to sigh, "I can't remember the Michael who was in those silly flicks."

"It's not entirely fair to say they were silly." Lauren crossed her arms, "They were different from the movies that wanted to be shallow or just plain crude. It always seemed your first few films had a lot of heart. Somehow I imagined that meant you did too."

Michael felt sucker punched. How many times had he heard this from his brother? Or his agent? The critics and fans said similar things over the years. "Comedies don't get awards, have you noticed? You have to do something challenging, make people face reality."

"Maybe the reason people go to a comedy is they have too much reality. Isn't it rather arrogant to presume that your audience doesn't?"

Michael sat back and glared at Lauren. "You don't always have to tell me what you think. I wish you would hold back just a tiny bit."

Lauren snapped, "Listen, if you think you're responsible for giving us poor mortals a dose of reality, maybe you're the one who isn't facing it."

Obviously a nerve had been touched. However, he was annoyed as well. He sensed he should back off. She was ready to attack, and the last time that happened, he attacked back stupidly.

"Point taken. You were thrown a lot of reality at a young

age. How did you handle it?" Maybe this wasn't the time or place to ask, but it was something he wanted to know from the time they first started talking.

Lauren drained her glass of water, "Do you remember when you came to the obedience class and the one dog wouldn't stop fighting me? That's exactly how I was, only I was fighting God. Just like that dog chose to trust rather than keep fighting, I did the same thing. Fighting wasn't working so well, but as soon as I gave up and decided to trust the One who understood all of our lives better than I could, things turned around for me. Tyler came to this conclusion much sooner than I did. That's what got my attention."

Michael grimaced, "I can't say I am all on board for the God thing."

"Why would you be? You're already worshipped and live in your own version of Heaven." Lauren smirked.

Maybe he should have stuck with antagonizing her. She was agitating him in a different way and he felt irritated. "Are you sure that isn't a cop out? I mean, it wasn't that easy for you."

"No, it wasn't easy at all. Trust me, I was angry for a long time. If I could have grabbed God by the lapels and demanded an answer, I would have done it."

"You weren't afraid of being struck by lightning?"

"You really don't know about God do you?"

"So you got your answer?"

"No, but I got Jesus. That was better." Lauren took her

money out and Michael quickly motioned for her to put it away.

Michael shifted in his seat, "You weren't just collapsed in a heap?"

"Sometimes. But tears can bring clearer vision." Lauren sighed, "As much as I don't want to admit it, Franny forcing me back to Bible study helped me to remember that."

"Too many rules. I couldn't do it," Michael looked out the window.

"You know the beauty of Jesus is that once we're forgiven, we don't have to worry about not measuring up to an impossible standard anymore. It's the best freedom in the world."

The two stood and headed for the counter to pay Raylene, who was more occupied with her phone than the two of them. Lauren turned to him, "I'm sure the God stuff doesn't make a lot of sense to you. But seriously, it's real. I was too angry to be changed by something that wasn't."

He was done with this subject, "This is some heavy stuff."

Lauren must have read the expression on his face. She nodded and touched his arm, "Dinner was heavy enough." She patted her belly with a smile and the two of them left.

*

After their meal, Michael dropped Lauren off and headed for the theater. Country living must be catching up with him–he was ready to turn in by eight o'clock and, instead, rehearsal was just about to start. He remembered when he didn't even have dinner until eight o'clock. Now he was one of those early birds. Yikes.

However, the students always amused him. While the range of talent among the cast was vast, they all seemed to be happy to be part of the production. That was something Michael found to be rare in his world. The camaraderie among the film talent and crew was nonexistent. The actors often stayed in their own trailers, far away from everyone else. It was much more of an individual experience. Sometimes that wasn't the case, but the trajectory was.

Michael found himself engrossed in the scene from *Our Town* with Monty playing George and Pam playing Emily.

Monty was on the stage, over emoting, "I'm celebrating because I've got a friend who tells me all the things that I ought to be told me."

Pam's lines were smoother as she spoke Emily's words, "George, please don't think of that. I don't know why I said it. It's not true."

Just then the lights strayed off the actors, stopping the action. As Jim rose to address the issue, Monty and Pam fell out of character and chatted. Michael stretched, his long legs cramped in the theater seats.

With Monty's back to him, it was hard to be sure, but Michael thought he heard him say something to Pam about 'that Kelly.' This kid must have it bad for her.

"Hey Mickey," Monty called to him, "did you ever do this play?"

Michael nodded, "Sure. When I was in high school."

"See? I told you it was old," Monty hissed at Pam.

It was an amateur mistake for Monty to think the sound wouldn't carry from the stage. He chose to ignore it. Instead, he decided to offer some perspective, "Monty, instead of acting while you say the words, think about them and then move according to their meaning. Think about what George just told Emily. He's saying that her honesty makes him a stronger person, and he's grateful for the honesty. When Emily tries to deflect it, don't let her do so easily."

Monty nodded, but Michael wasn't too sure he really understood the point. However, when Jim resolved the issue and the actors reset, the scene did indeed flow more smoothly. Michael no longer felt tired but energized. This is what he lived for–his life blood.

Chapter Nineteen–The Learning Curve

"Anyone have any problems or triumphs this week you'd like to share?"

Franny raised her hand, "Goliath was doing so well with me and now all of a sudden it's like he doesn't even respond to his own name."

"Most dogs experience a learning curve. What you're describing is normal. You may notice that they do just what you've taught them for weeks. Suddenly, they become idiots."

Lauren shot Michael a look. He made the connection. He smirked back. Very funny. Inwardly he groaned. What was it going to take to get her to ease up?

Then she grinned at him before turning back to her class, "Don't lose your patience with them. They need you now more than ever. Hang with them–they'll get it." She tossed him another look before putting the class through some drills.

After the last of the owners and dogs left, Lauren heard Michael on his phone.

He stood with his back to her, looking out the window. "Look, you made it clear you don't need me. I see no reason to help you now."

Lauren stayed silent. She could tell by his stiff stance he was irritated. As he listened to whatever the other person said, she heard him sigh quietly. "Listen, you don't want to meet with that guy. You know his reputation."

He was quiet some more. Lauren slipped behind the desk and pretended to be absorbed with paper work. Of course she wasn't. She listened to every word he said and kept an eye on him.

Finally he took two quick steps and stopped, "Kelly, you should have listened to what I was trying to tell you all along. Not that you're going to listen to this either, but here's my last piece of advice. Don't mess with crazy people."

After a few more testy exchanges, he put away his phone and turned around. Lauren pretended to type something into the computer. It was a horrible reminder of the other life that really belonged to Michael. The life that was the complete opposite of what hers was in this place.

*

Mixed emotions went well with the mixed salad Lauren prepared to take to Alice and Jim's that night. Michael was coming too. Yes, all the markings of a double date and they all were pretending it wasn't. Did it have to be? Couldn't it just be adults enjoying time together? Would Lauren never be able to enjoy the company of males without it being misconstrued?

But deep down, she looked forward to the time. How could she not? Michael amused her, and goodness knows she needed to be amused. Her dark thoughts threatened her still, though it was much worse during Tyler's illness. Still, she missed laughing, and Michael made her laugh.

As Michael and Jim sipped drinks on the front porch of Lauren and Jim's home, Lauren worked around the kids' toys that were strewn around the living areas. When she went to place a fork at a place setting, she almost slipped on a plastic car.

Alice tsked in disgust, "There is always one more thing. I put it all away, then those darn kiddos sneak back in here."

"At least they like to play," Lauren commented, setting the toy in the large basket with the others.

"Don't we all?" Alice said, placing Lauren's salad on the table. "How are the home repairs going?"

Lauren glanced over her shoulder to make sure Michael couldn't hear, "Great. That downspout is the only thing left. My 'to do' list has never been so short."

The two women joined the men. Michael handed Lauren a glass of iced tea. "Thanks, Ty."

Michael paused, quickly glancing at Alice, who was nervously looking between Jim and Lauren. Clearly she was unaware as she sipped her tea. Noticing the stares of everyone except Michael, she asked, "What?"

"Jim, why don't you and Michael get seated at the table while Lauren helps me bring in our meal?"

Lauren followed Alice, her brows knitted in confusion.

"What's up?" She whispered when they were in the kitchen.

"You didn't notice?"

"That Michael winked at me? He does that. Don't make a big deal of it."

Alice picked up a serving bowl, "Actually I did miss that. But you called him Ty."

Lauren leaned against the counter, her face pale.

"It's okay, Lauren," Alice tried to console her. "It doesn't mean anything."

Lauren sat down and took a deep breath, "Maybe it does. Maybe I'm forgetting Tyler."

Dinner went on, but Lauren was rattled, picking at her food the best she could. Her appetite disappeared entirely. She made every effort to appear normal and she hoped it was working. Despite her intentions, following the conversation was difficult.

"Pam seems to be growing into the parts very well," Jim raved.

Michael agreed, adding, "Monty has really grown. His agony over Emily is so real. He executed that graveyard scene perfectly."

"Maybe executed is the wrong word," Alice snorted, all except Lauren laughed.

"That's the fun of acting–you get to experience so many emotions."

"Yet stay a safe distance from them," Lauren piped in.

Michael disagreed, "Not necessarily. To do a really effective job, you really get into them."

"What are some of your favorite roles you've played, Mick?" Jim asked.

"That's easy. I loved playing the president. When I was young, I wanted to be president, so acting like it was probably better than actually being one."

Lauren dropped her fork. "You mean to tell me that you actually felt the weight of responsibility for the free world on your shoulders?"

Alice gave her a look, which she ignored. Michael seemed nonplussed. "I did a lot of research and talked to people."

"Research?" Lauren said, her voice rising. "You have a conversation and think you know how it feels to really suffer?"

Michael looked at Jim, who looked at Alice. She put her hand on Lauren's, "Don't take this where it shouldn't go."

Lauren shrugged it off. "After spending time with me, do you really think you could give a reasonable rendition of what it's like to watch a young man turn old and wither before your eyes?"

Michael leaned forward, his consoling tone not working, "That's not entirely what I'm saying."

Lauren stood, tossing the napkin on the table, "You have no idea. And you can't. Acting is a game that fools you into thinking you know something. But you don't."

With that, Lauren stomped out of the dining room and out

of the house. Fortunately it was a short walk to her own home. Maybe by then her anger might dissipate. Why did everyone say things like, "I know how you feel" when they had no idea? No one knew. Chicken casseroles and flirtation, even getting rid of the evidence of Tyler's existence wouldn't change that.

What they didn't understand was Tyler was a man. She was human as well. The mistakes she made, the distance she kept from Tyler, the relief she felt from the stress being over. But worst of all, she wasn't by his side when he died. She was just so ashamed. Maybe they understood loss, but they couldn't understand her hard heart.

The knock on her door put a pit into her stomach. She didn't want to explain herself right now. However, with a window on her front door, it was hard to ignore Guinness' enthusiasm at seeing Michael.

She opened the door, deciding to let him speak first. He carried a folder that he nervously tapped in his other hand.

"Listen, you're right that I can't pretend to know what you felt then or what you are feeling now," he said.

"Not even close," Lauren snapped.

"I'm not trying to replace Tyler. It sounds like no one could do that." He handed her the folder, "But you may want to be careful how you play that widow card."

Lauren snapped her head to meet his gaze. He wasn't angry. He meant it. Still. "What's that supposed to mean?"

"I found this in the cabin. It seemed important for you to have it."

She could feel him looking at her as she read the tab of the folder, 'Letter of Recommendation.'

"Is this a joke?" She accused.

"Didn't seem like it to me." With that, Michael left.

Lauren closed the door and walked to the table. Guinness sniffed the folder with interest. He couldn't still detect the scent of Tyler, could he? Lauren sank into the chair and read it. She alternated between laughter and tears. She read it twice, whispering the last part, *"Lauren filled my life with joy. I hope I slip away when she's not around. Eventually she will remember the good years we had before this illness. In short, I could never find the words to adequately explain the character of Lauren Sanders."*

Collapsing in a wave of tears that hit her hard, Lauren laid her head on the table and sobbed. "Thank you. Oh, thank you."

Lynne E. Scott

Chapter Twenty–The Pressure of Being the Alpha Dog

As Lauren stacked the bucket of dog food, two boxes of treats, a large bin of toys, raised dog bowls and deluxe dog beds that belonged to the owner of three feisty dachshunds, she thought of the letter. Maybe she didn't give herself enough credit for what Tyler saw. It wasn't like she doubted his love for her. Maybe she doubted that he knew she loved him. Now she knew. He'd felt loved. That was the most important thing she'd wanted to know before he died. Despite her exhaustion, when she worried love was just another item on her things to do list, Tyler knew he was loved.

The three dogs yipped at the end of their leashes as their owner's car pulled into the driveway. Lauren smiled. How dogs knew their own vehicle never ceased to amuse her.

As the owner packed up their items, she asked Lauren, "Do you think there's anything to that whole alpha-dog theory?"

"Some dog behaviorists don't believe in it. But I've seen these three brothers in action and there's clearly a fight for dominance when it's time to eat."

The owner nodded, "Yes, and you should see them with

toys. But Mel never participates. He just watches Ned and Sam duke it out."

Lauren grinned, "And I wouldn't say Mel is a wimp. He seems pretty content to not fight all the time. Not everyone can be the top dog."

As the owner put the dogs in their crate in the car, she thanked Lauren, "That's true. There's peace in not fighting for control all the time."

*

"So rubber duckies are still a thing," Michael muttered as he laid in the large tub at the cabin. The yellow duck was under the vanity, along with some seriously crusted Epsom salts. His muscles ached from a full day of chopping wood at Lauren's. He squeaked the toy twice, causing Guinness to poke his nose through the ajar door. Michael tossed the dog the toy. The dog picked it up in his mouth, squeaked it once, then dropped it and walked away.

"That was fun," Michael allowed his head to sink under the water. It was eons since he took a leisurely bath, particularly in an old tub large enough to accommodate his height. Of course it was that long since he'd performed such physical labor. The last time his muscles ached this much was when he had to hold onto the side of a boat in cold, rainy weather for a scene in a movie. He never did like that director. Then a massage therapist worked his soreness out. He used to be so pampered.

Every now and then a fleeting urgency filled him when he worried that if he didn't return to his work soon, he would be completely irrelevant. It didn't take long now. There always was a younger pup vying to take an old dog's place. Michael smiled. Lauren's training classes must be getting to him.

Tom, his agent, assured him that he may have a longer shelf life since a couple of his earlier movies were labeled as "iconic." Still, life moved faster now. Respect wasn't part of the younger generation's vocabulary.

Did he just think 'younger generation?' He groaned and resurfaced, his aches reminding him that he was definitely aging. Yes, he needed to think about a well-timed return. The letter he gave Lauren seemed like a good idea at the time. But she was out of sight all day, which was unlike her. Just as he considered toweling off, he heard what sounded like a door closing. Sitting up, he listened, but didn't hear Guinness bark. That dog was certainly good at protecting. No one would enter with that dog around.

Slowly, he stood and toweled off. Another sound, like a floor creaking, caused him to freeze. Michael put the towel around his waist and tiptoed to the door. He was pretty sure this was how most slasher movies started, telling from the recent bit part he played in a series of horror movies. He hated those films, but his part paid well.

As Michael came down the hall, he saw the intruder. Guinness stood by her, wagging his tail as she rummaged through the closet on her knees, her bottom facing him. Michael carefully considered its shape, then tried to decide what to do. He picked up the rubber ducky the dog dropped and beaned Lauren in the rear. The yellow toy squeaked perfectly as it bounced off her, making Guinness dive after it.

Lauren yipped and turned around. Her expression was

priceless. Guilty. Michael laughed, "Now who's trespassing?"

From Lauren's blush, he remembered he still was wearing only a towel. She looked away, which made Michael smile more.

"Now, Mickey, I was only…" she tried.

"Oh, now it's Mickey is it?"

"Could you please put on some clothes?" Lauren begged.

"Not until you tell me why you're here." He could see she was growing frustrated, but he wasn't ready to let her off the hook just yet.

"You had no business reading that letter."

"I know and I didn't mean to read it," Michael replied. "But come on, it isn't like there's a plethora of reading material around here."

Lauren finally turned to look at him, a grin tugging at her lips, "Plethora? Your vocabulary matches your nosiness. Now could you please get dressed?"

"What's wrong with the towel? I bet I look really good in it," Michael read Lauren's feigned annoyance and could tell she was amused. "Is the reason you broke into your cabin to yell at me?"

"I knocked and called in but no one answered. So I walked in."

"I must have been underwater," Michael said.

"What?" Lauren asked.

"So you walked in and decided to rifle through the closet. That seems pretty nosy to me."

Lauren looked like a helpless child sitting on the floor. "I just wondered if there was more."

Michael softened. "Nothing that would be quite as interesting. That box has a few more of his things, like his Bible. But give me a minute."

Once in his tiny bedroom, he garbed himself in whatever clothing he could find to hurry back to her. She was sitting on the couch petting Guinness when he returned. He wasn't sure of how clean his clothes were, but at least he smelled good.

She looked up at him accusingly, "Has my dog been bothering you?"

"Not as much as you have," Michael teased. "It's been nice having him come down now and then. Plus, I don't have to worry about gun-toting dog trainers."

"Yes, you do," Lauren grinned back. She noticed the opened game box on the coffee table and reached for the cards. "I had no idea we left so much around. And here you are nosing through all of it."

Michael couldn't quite read her tone. He sat on the other end of the couch and looked her in the eye, "The mistake I made was not asking you about the box. But Tyler left you a wonderful gift with that letter. You may also want to go through his Bible. I'm assuming it's his handwriting in the margins and passages he underlined."

Lauren blanched and fished it out of the box. "Are you

telling me you actually read the Bible?"

"Just the good parts," Michael smiled at her. "Now, how about we move on from here?"

Lauren seemed to accept this and picked up the cards. "Conversation Cards. I always liked this game." She presented the deck to him face down, "Pick one."

He took one and read the question on the other side, "What board game best describes you?"

"I hate this question," Lauren frowned and thought a moment, "You answer first."

"Risk," Michael said, like a challenge.

Lauren raised an eyebrow at him, "I suppose mine is Monopoly." They both laughed, their manner suddenly much more relaxed. She took a card and read it, "If you could date any celebrity, who would it be?"

Michael snorted, "If?" He scratched his head as if this was the most perplexing question of the century, "This is hardly a level playing field. You answer. And you can't say me."

"I could never date you. It would require a whole new wardrobe," Lauren said with absolute sincerity. "Jimmy Stewart seemed solid, except I didn't like his voice. I like a deep, growly voice."

Michael leaned in, putting an arm awkwardly around her shoulders, "You mean like mine?"

"More like Gregory Peck or Cary Grant," she answered, tossing his arm away from her.

"Why do you pick all the dead guys?" Michael said flippantly, then winced.

He was grateful she was forgiving, "It's okay. I guess they are safer, aren't they?"

"Would Tyler want you to live a safe life?" he took her hand, hoping she wouldn't pull it away.

Lauren's face twisted in emotion, "Despite what that letter said, I can't. I can't want someone else."

He gave her hand a squeeze, "You may decide that now, but you may want to un-decide it later."

Lauren stared at their entwined hands, but didn't withdraw hers. Finally, she said, "I've got dog class."

Michael looked at her meaningfully, "You can really destroy the moment, you know that?"

She stood and headed for the door. Turning, she half smiled, "I am fully aware of it. That's part of the problem."

After she was gone, he wondered what she meant. However, he could still spend time with her. He walked over to Franny Bottoms' home to get Goliath.

Lynne E. Scott

Chapter Twenty-one–The Blind Tunnel

As the owners and dogs circled around Lauren, she called out the description of the exercise they were about to attempt. "As you'll see, we're going to try a few new things in our obstacle course today. You have the teeter totter, which is difficult for dogs to walk over. The unsteady nature of the object causes them to jump off. They are no fools–they don't want to fall."

She walked over and pointed at it, while Scout followed, "Teeter!" Scout obediently ran over the object, from end to end, only one small hesitation slowing him.

"And over here we have the blind tunnel," Lauren walked over to a chute that had cloth at the one end. "This tunnel is one of the hardest obstacles for a dog. As with the teeter totter, dogs don't like to go through something when they can't see the other side. They like to see the end before they start it. However, if you stand at the other end and call to them, they will risk the darkness in order to see you. Remember, they trust you."

Lauren gave a hand signal to Scout to sit and stay. As she walked to the opposite end, Michael looked at the assembled group. They watched as if she was performing a magic act. She crouched down where Scout could no longer see her. She called him and he shot through the tunnel, the fabric of the chute rustling as he exited. Some of the owners clapped.

"The dogs often want to back out of the tunnel. But when they go through to the other side, where you'll be waiting, their confidence soars." Lauren looked around the room. "And confidence is exactly what most dogs need, particularly if they've been abused or neglected in any way."

Then Lauren walked over to Michael. Grabbing the leash from him, Lauren gave him a steady look.

"Come on Goliath," Lauren stood at the open end of the tunnel and pointed at Michael to go to the blind end. He stood and looked at her. She cocked her head to the side in expectation. When he didn't move, she pointed at the floor, "Sit!" The class laughed, and Michael grinned.

"Call your dog!"

Michael kneeled down on the uncomfortable concrete, "Goliath, come!"

Nothing.

He heard Lauren say softly, "Call him again."

He stretched closer to the opening of the chute and yelled a little louder, "Goliath, come!"

Still nothing. The class teetered in merriment.

"This time, try calling him more enthusiastically instead of yelling. Act like he's missing a big party. Bang your hands on the ground. The poor little dog is sitting at my feet bored to death."

He would get her back for this. But Michael did as he was told, hitting his hands on either side of the chute, calling the dog's name in a ridiculously high voice. He was practically lying on the ground now, his face inches from the end of the chute as he shouted for the dog.

Just then the dog emerged and touched Michael's nose with his own. They both seemed surprised, which delighted the group. Michael scooped up the little dog, once again feeling the invigoration of a cheering crowd. Would he never get past being the center of attention? He secretly enjoyed it more than a person should.

*

Why he gave in to Lauren's request to attend the local Pork Rind Festival was beyond him. It was just wrong on so many levels. He never went into crowds like this, and a celebration of fried pig skin? Lauren insisted it was worth going, beyond people watching. She got in his car, the familiar long-sleeved shirt over her shoulders, "Expecting it to get cold?" he asked.

Lauren looked at the shirt and shrugged, "It's my favorite."

When they arrived on the main street of the small town, Michael noticed all the families milling around a park and picnic area. As they walked past a number of booths on each side of the street, they passed a space where three deep fryers busily made fresh pork rinds for a short line of customers.

"What is up with the pork rind?" Michael whispered to Lauren.

"Hey, we have to celebrate something. Haven't you heard

the phrase 'for every animal and vegetable a festival'?" she asked.

"No, I can't say I have. Small town living is really expanding my horizons."

Michael noticed Lauren relaxing the more they walked about. People greeted her with a friendly wave. "You're really popular here."

Lauren shook her head, "It's not popularity. It's just a small town where people know each other."

As if to prove her point, a small boy walking by holding hands with his mother pointed at Lauren and said, "Hi Dog Lady!"

"Hi Jake!" Lauren waved back, smiling at Michael, "Don't say a word!"

Michael shrugged as if falsely accused.

"It's almost a relief to be called Dog Lady. Before I only was referred to as 'Tyler's wife.' At least I have my own identity, even if it's weird." Lauren smirked.

The two of them walked toward an area where men tended large grills with chicken halves on them. A long line weaved through some tables, which they joined.

"What's up with this?" Michael asked, pointing to a large mayonnaise jar half full of dollar bills and change.

"This is a fund-raiser for Sammy Walter, who is fighting a rare form of cancer," Lauren said, handing him a Styrofoam food tray.

"You mean this is going to raise enough money to pay their bills?"

Lauren shot him a look as volunteers scooped potato salad into the tray's compartment and applesauce in another. "Not even close. However, the family can see how much we care about them. These chicken dinners are pretty popular for fundraisers."

As a barbecued half chicken was placed on the last empty compartment of Michael's tray, he wondered at the practice. He never heard of such a thing before.

Once they were done eating, Michael followed Lauren over to a young child sitting in a wheel chair. A scarf was wrapped around the child's head, which Lauren admired while she knelt down. Michael felt awkward and had no idea what to say. Fortunately, his celebrity connections may pay off if he could come up with an idea.

"Hey, Tiger, how about a Nascar driver autograph?" He felt proud with this suggestion, since he noticed several booths at the festival featured Nascar themed goods.

The child looked confused. "My brother might like that, I guess."

Lauren whispered to Michael, "Sammy's a girl."

"Oh," Michael knelt down by the child, determined to get it right, "What do you like?"

"Malibu Barbie!" Sammy brightened.

Lauren busted with laughter, and gave Sammy's shoulder a

squeeze, "I believe he has many of those."

Michael, to his surprise, was embarrassed. They both said good bye to the child after Lauren promised to deliver on Sammy's wish. She was still laughing when they ran into a stern looking woman.

Lauren's demeanor completely changed, "Oh, hi, Carly."

"I thought that was you, Lauren," Carly sniped, "So, you two are a 'thing' then? Kind of soon, isn't it?" She gave Michael a quick scan from head to toe.

"No, we're not dating, Carly." Lauren began.

Michael placed an arm over Lauren's shoulders and pulled her close, "That's right. Dating is far too formal of a word for our relationship." He kissed Lauren's neck, noticing Carly's look of horror, then Lauren's look of surprise.

Carly huffed and shot Michael a dirty look. Before marching off, she snapped, "Lauren always did take in strays."

Michael didn't drop his arm from Lauren's shoulders. "So much for the friendly small town vibe."

Lauren's irritation showed, "Why would she be so nasty? It's not any of her business, but do people expect me to stay single forever?"

Her feistiness was attractive. Instead of trying to calm her down, he decided to feed the fire, "Absolutely. You have every right to live. Who was she, anyhow?"

Lauren didn't answer but she did shrug off Michael's arm. Just as he wondered what he'd done wrong, she took off the long-sleeved shirt and tied it around her waist. Then she looked him in the eye and grabbed his hand, pulling him as she walked forward.

People were not subtle noticing this. Lauren didn't seem to care. Michael noticed Monty and some of the other college kids at a picnic table, most of them preoccupied with texting. Monty waved with one hand, his phone in the other. Michael waved back. There was just something about that kid he didn't like.

He wasn't sure that Lauren was aware of the people who turned to look at them as they passed, but he was starting to get the old irritation he got with the paparazzi. He stopped and pulled Lauren toward him, "Let's go. How about we go out for a nice dinner tonight? At some place that doesn't have laminated menus."

"I'm not really up for driving an hour away," Lauren laughed.

"Someday?" Michael asked.

Lauren looked down, her cheeks turning a light shade of pink. Finally, she nodded.

Michael felt like he was a teenager again. And so did Lauren.

Lynne E. Scott

Chapter Twenty-two–Puppy Love

The next morning, Michael walked into the kennel office as Lauren played with a young puppy. Looking up, Lauren felt her heart do that warming thing. If it wasn't so wonderful, she might be more annoyed.

The pup was adorable with the way it stumbled over its gangly legs. Seeing Michael, it loped over to him and threw itself against his legs. Lauren chuckled to herself, thinking that throwing herself at Michael was exactly what she felt like doing as well. She quickly checked herself. While he acted friendly around her, she knew that she was hardly someone he would take seriously. And she couldn't afford to waste too much emotional energy on someone who was going to leave.

As the puppy rolled on its back, Michael gave it a good rubbing, "You must love puppies."

Lauren shook her head, "Not really. I don't have puppy love very often. They are a lot of work. Give me an old dog any day. They are loyal and dignified."

Lauren watched as Michael picked up the dog, only to have the pup wriggle and grunt. Michael set her back down in front of Lauren, "that's too much enthusiasm for me."

"She's in my puppy class and she's still working on this." Lauren gently laid the dog on her side and quietly said, "Settle." The pup's eyes looked at Lauren, but the limbs that had been in constant motion stilled. "Good Delilah. Okay!" The pup shot back up at the release command.

"What does settle help them learn?" Michael asked, trying the same technique with the pup.

"For one thing, the vet's office appreciates a dog that can settle," Lauren said as she watched Delilah comply with Michael's command. "But, most importantly, learning to settle introduces calm and self-control into the dog's life."

Michael released Delilah and gave her a treat. "Self-control? I can't think of anything more counter cultural."

"Not when we're constantly told to indulge," Lauren watched as Delilah raced toward Guinness, climbing and tumbling over the large dog.

Guinness got up with a sigh and walked away. Lauren picked up the puppy, "Okay, enough fun and games for a while."

"You're both troopers if you ask me," Michael said, shaking his head.

As Lauren entered the kennel and put the pup in its run, she smiled. Normally she wouldn't find being called a trooper a compliment. However, she understood what Michael was trying to say to her. It meant a lot.

*

Michael's anger boiled as he looked at Kelly's latest video. Why did he even watch it?

Kelly sat in a trendy bar, sipping a trendy cocktail. She preened for the camera and enthused about her favorite lipstick, who the summer's hottest actor would be, and finally a tease for a video she was about to play.

It was Michael and Lauren holding hands, walking at the festival. Snorting to herself, she said, "How far our friend Mickey Quinlan has fallen. It looks like he's dating Ellie Mae Clampett. At a festival for pigs!"

Michael tossed the phone aside. What had he done to Lauren? He couldn't drag her into this pit, not when he was just starting to feel like he was getting free from it. Maybe it wouldn't bother her. Maybe she was trusting him a bit more.

They were supposed to go out to dinner tonight. He'd tell her then, just not make a big deal about it. "By the way, Lauren, you may be on the cover of a tabloid." Then he thought about it again. He probably wasn't tabloid material anymore. At least not front page. Still, he needed to let her know.

He shook his head in disgust as he thought of the stupidity of it all. Talk about obstacles.

*

Lauren stared at her jewelry box, wondering when the last time she wore something nice might have been. Possibly the funeral. Ugh. With one enjoyable evening under their belts, Michael asked to take her "somewhere nice." It was likely that Michael's definition of someplace nice was much different from hers.

She looked down at her jeans which were stained with formula for a kitten dumped at her house. Fortunately, the little foundling took to bottle feeding quickly. How could people do that to a helpless kitten? If she hadn't heard the mews, or her cats or dogs were aggressive, the feline would never have survived.

The sleeping kitten was in a cardboard box at her feet. She wondered at the feelings of tenderness she felt for the kitten. Why couldn't she have been more like that when Tyler needed her? When he wanted her to sit and watch a movie with him, she opted instead to sneak upstairs and catch a nap. She was so tired. But now it was too late to ever watch a movie with him. Had he thought she was cruel? Had he known time was slipping away and felt neglected? When she thought of it, she got all torn up inside.

And what was she thinking, going on a date with a movie star? Life sure was surreal. What was Michael thinking? Possibly, the exact same thing.

She sighed and picked up the kitten, cuddling it in her arms. She leaned back against the bathroom vanity and closed her eyes, the purrs calming her. Okay, Lauren, try to focus.

There was only one dress that might work for this occasion, so she dug into the back of her closet to find it. It was a sheer coral color, and was cut in a way that managed to hide her body's flaws and enhance whatever limited assets she possessed.

With one last pat to her hair, she slipped on some high heels and evaluated her appearance. Honestly, she wasn't used to seeing herself like this person. She actually looked together. Maybe even pretty.

The dogs alerted her to Michael's presence. They no longer barked at him, but whined and wagged their tails. Lauren opened the door, her knees weak when she saw Michael shaved and dressed up. He looked amazing. This didn't explain why she suddenly wanted to cry.

With a big smile, Michael presented her with a bouquet of flowers he'd hidden behind his back. It was the stuff of romantic movies of forty years ago. Or corny commercials. Either way, Lauren felt her brave front crumble.

With her hand over her mouth, she began to sob. Inside, something felt like it broke. The last thing she remembered was Michael encircling her in his arms and pulling her close.

The next thing she knew, she was sitting on the back porch, her shoes off, Michael's tie loose, and a box of pizza in front of her.

"Did I pass out?" she asked.

"Maybe. You sort of stared into space for a long time after your crying jag. Dare I ask what that was about?" Michael said, opening a beer and pouring half of it into a glass for her.

"As soon as I figure it out, I may tell you. Sorry to mess things up."

Guinness walked over to Michael and jabbed him with a toy. Lauren snapped her fingers at him so he'd back off.

Michael looked at her then tossed the toy for the dog, who

happily chased it. "He's fine."

Lauren shook her head, "I can't believe he plays ball with you."

"Why?"

"He only played with Ty. He never played with me. He still doesn't," Lauren sighed.

"Maybe you're just not any fun," Michael said, throwing the ball again.

She stood to lean against the rails. Michael joined her, looking out over the pond. The bullfrogs croaked, one answering another. "Those frogs sure are a happy bunch," Michael grinned.

"Sometimes I hear them and think…."

"You're jealous?"

Lauren blushed and faced away as Michael teased her, "Come on! That embarrassed you?"

She felt Michael's arms pull her close, turning her face to look at him. Her heart fluttered. He leaned in and kissed her gently. She stiffened a little, but when he stopped and looked her in the eyes, she relaxed, a timid smile back at him.

It was all he needed, kissing her again, tentatively at first, but then with more intensity. This time when he pulled back to look at her, he seemed to look for her permission. She was sure. As she initiated the next kiss, she felt certain he sensed it as well.

As their passion grew, Lauren remembered the power, the

bliss. She shuddered. Michael caressed her shoulder, a discreet pass around her breasts. He stopped and looked at her questioningly. She giggled, "Did you forget what real ones feel like?"

She could tell by his expression it was true. She shook her head in disbelief, "What kind of world do you live in? Are there no women with their real body parts?"

"When I see you, I can see real beauty," he replied. "Thank you."

As Lauren pulled his head down to hers for a kiss, she didn't ask for what he was grateful. She could guess. She felt the same way.

Lynne E. Scott

Chapter Twenty-three–Leave It

Michael watched Lauren with the obedience group. Franny Bottoms decided to take Goliath through the remaining classes. It seemed Goliath listened to everyone except Franny. Lauren told her repeatedly that dog training was really owner training, but Franny still seemed worried about hurting the dog's feelings.

Lauren had a way of being direct with people without completely offending them. In Michael's world, people were indirect, often sugar coating criticism or even a suggestion to a point that left him wondering what exactly a person meant. No wonder he struggled with reality.

Scout watched Lauren as she told him "Leave it," then dropped a treat in front of him. The dog stared at the treat, a drizzle of saliva falling from his mouth.

Lauren directed her comments back to the group, "The 'leave it' command can save your dog's life. It can be used to tell your dog to stay away from a dead animal on the road, a baby's toy, another dog. Anything they shouldn't have." Looking back at Scout, she said, "Okay." The dog dove at the treat, devouring it in one gulp.

The class laughed. One man said, "Hey, can I use that on my wife when she gets near the cheesecake?"

Lauren laughed along with the group, "Remember this is the woman you sleep next to, Mr. Jacobs. She may use the 'leave it' command on you!"

With that, she worked through the group as they practiced the drill. Michael watched with admiration. She was at ease. Sometimes he felt like he couldn't function in a group without a script anymore. For the most part, his environment was controlled. He simply didn't rub elbows with people he didn't know anymore. In his world, it was nearly impossible to move in public without it creating a small scene. Or at least it used to be. He seemed to be doing okay in this tiny town. They treated him like he was just a regular person.

He envied Lauren's world, which seemed odd. He felt protective of her, particularly in light of the conversation he had late last night with Kelly.

When he heard from Tom about the pictures she'd posted, he called her and asked her to leave Lauren out of it. "Whatever is or was between you and me doesn't involve her."

"Oh, aren't you ever the hero?" Kelly sneered. "Fine. I'll agree if you do one thing for me."

The details of what Kelly wanted made him feel ill. At the same time, they seemed necessary. He didn't know how to break it to Lauren. It didn't help when she sauntered over to him after the owners and dogs left. He could tell she was feeling sassy and carefree. Since it was something he hoped to see in her for a long time, it was killing him to tell her what was coming next. Maybe he could delay it.

"So," Lauren said, putting her hands on his shoulders. "Do you think we'll make it to the restaurant this time? I'm pretty sure I can dress up without freaking out this time."

Michael closed his eyes. How was he going to do this? "About that. I have to go home."

Lauren struggled with his meaning, "Sure, you can go home and change."

"No, home away from this home." Michael felt punched in the gut by the look of hurt in her eyes. "It's just some quick work stuff I need to do. I'll be back."

Later when he packed his bag, he remembered the way she silently walked to the door with him, how she slipped into that old shirt of hers before walking away from him without one word. But if only she knew what Kelly could do to turn her life upside down, maybe she wouldn't be angry with him. Maybe.

*

Lauren tossed and turned all night. How could she be so stupid? He was an actor. A professional at faking emotions and she fell for it. Of course he was going back to his world. What did she expect? Nothing here would keep him. What was worth sticking around for? Or who?

The next morning, Lauren fussed with the plants on her back porch. The greenery thrived. She wished she felt the same. To keep the flowering plants going, she removed the spent flowers, their glory well past.

Alice came around the corner and greeted her in her lighthearted way. Even though Lauren felt wretched, Alice's mood always raised her spirits. Plus, her friend was an excellent worker, grabbing a hose and tending to the dry plants. "So how was your big date?"

"It was more like a near-date experience." Lauren answered. No matter how much she may want to avoid this conversation, it was inevitable.

Alice shrugged, "Maybe next time."

"That's the thing, there won't be a next time." Lauren didn't look up from the flower pot, "He went back to California."

"Oh," Alice said, "Jim said he was going to be gone for a couple days. But I didn't know he was already gone."

"He was vague about what was going on. Something about a movie."

"Well, it is his career."

Lauren wanted to blurt out that just once she would be considered worthy of sticking around for, but that seemed overly dramatic. Instead she tried to be nonchalant, "He said he was thinking of quitting."

Alice replied, "You can't think that walking away from his whole life and career would be easy."

"No, I guess not," Lauren sighed. "But I should have known that. I mean, maybe I'm just too stupid to date."

"That's not it," Alice teased. "Is he a good kisser?"

"Yes," Lauren melted, "Yes he is." Then she railed, "Darn it, Alice! Who does he think he is? I didn't ask for any of this. And here I am, suckered in by him. Why would he mess with me? Honestly, what kind of person is he after all?"

A stream of water socked Lauren in the face. Alice grinned as she turned the hose away, "Stop. The world didn't end did it? Even if nothing else happened, the world didn't end because you kissed another man."

*

For the second time, Michael wondered why he was in California, sitting by a very agog Kelly in a trendy restaurant, with a man named Cecil Mercury. Tom did his best to focus the conversation. It was hard when he didn't want to be there.

Michael assessed Cecil Mercury, noticing he looked like a product of the hippie generation who decided to become a mini mogul in the field of movie production. What a joke. This man was a caricature. The other diners kept glancing in their direction. Michael found himself longing for the greasy spoon diner in the middle of nowhere, pouring coffee for farmers. Maybe he had a fever.

Cecil's abrasive voice interrupted his thoughts, "Kelly, I saw your spread in Magnum. First class stuff."

Michael noticed the leer he gave Kelly, chatting her up. Kelly seemed to encourage more. Finally, Michael leaned over to Tom, "So this is what the bottom of the barrel feels like."

Tom shushed him, "Somehow I think this might work."

"And Mickey, your experience will definitely be an asset,"

Cecil chirped.

The comment rubbed him the wrong way, "What do you mean by experience?"

Tom interjected, "But is it a lead role?"

Cecil hesitated, "The troubadour role is essential."

Michael sat up straight, "Troubadour? What?" He eyed Kelly, who smiled smugly.

As Tom and Cecil talked further, Michael muttered to Kelly, "You really want to work for this guy?"

Kelly tossed her hair, "He says I have a post-modern Olivia Newton-John quality."

"Do you even know who Olivia Newton-John is?"

Kelly shot him a look of annoyance, "I looked her up."

"How's Jessica? She's the only friend of yours I could tolerate."

"I heard she's got cancer or something," Kelly looked around the restaurant to see who was seeing her, a pleasant expression stuck on her face.

Michael was revolted by how casually Kelly said this, "That's awful. What's her prognosis?"

"Her what?" Kelly looked at him, then caught herself, "How would I know? My life coach said to keep positive thoughts."

Ignoring this, Michael decided to get down to brass tacks. "So I'm here, like we agreed. No pictures flying around cyberspace okay?"

Kelly cozied up to him, "I knew you cared about me." Just as she kissed him, a man walked by and clicked a picture with his phone.

Michael struggled to be patient, "You saw him coming didn't you?"

"I'm learning to make the most of every opportunity," Kelly laughed.

Cecil's grating voice asked, "Mickey, I understand you can skate."

He couldn't take any more, "I'm skating? A skating troubadour? What is this–a remake of Xanadu?" He grabbed his coat and put on his sunglasses, "No way! I'm out!"

Just as he turned to walk away, he heard Kelly say, "It's a good thing you didn't mention the lederhosen."

Lynne E. Scott

Chapter Twenty-four–Can't Lose a Spark

Lauren felt like someone drove over her with a bus. Emotionally, she was sure that was what happened. As she stumbled around the grocery store picking out random foods, she wondered if she would ever feel happier for more than five minutes at a time.

Wendy and Martin came around the end of the aisle. So much for hoping she wouldn't run into anyone she knew.

"Sparky hasn't chewed up anything in three weeks," Martin gushed.

"I'm sorry I ever doubted you, Lauren," Wendy said, squeezing her arm. "We now have a well-behaved and happy dog. We had a lot of concerns early on."

"There's no 'we' about who was concerned!" Martin interrupted.

"Okay, I did. But Sparky still has his spark. In fact, he has a better spark than before." Wendy laughed, "You are quite the Dog Lady."

After they left, Lauren noted her new identity. Maybe being the Dog Lady wasn't a step up from being Tyler's Wife. But it was new and, most importantly, it was her own.

But was it enough?

Lauren made one more visit to the snack section and then set the assorted goods on the counter as Raylene rung them up, "It's amazin' what you can learn about a person's personal life by what they eat." She looked at the variety of bags of potato chips, "I'm pretty sure you forgot the onion flavored."

Lauren frowned, "I don't like that one." Her eyes fell to the trash magazines by the cash register. One featured a picture of Michael kissing Kelly in a restaurant. The headline screamed, "Look who's back together!"

"Wait," Lauren said, walking away and coming back with a tub of chocolate frosting.

"You must be havin' a bad day."

Lauren paid and grabbed her bags, muttering, "Groceries may reveal character, but not the way a headline can."

Once she got home, Lauren put away most of the junk food, save the item she craved the most. Sitting on the couch, she turned on what she hoped would be mindless television that did not include celebrity dirt. She settled on a show that took what looked to be junk and made it into treasure. To Lauren, it seemed hopefully redemptive.

A knock on the door forced her from her comfortable spot. She let Alice in, who seemed bent on disrupting her sulk.

"I really had you pegged as more of a Godiva girl."

Lauren frowned, then noticed the death grip she had on the

can of frosting with the spoon sticking out of it. "Desperation has not standards."

Alice nodded, "You saw the picture too, huh?"

Lauren sighed, sitting back down on the couch, "I worried the next man I would meet might have a latent terminal illness. What I didn't count on was terminal stupidity."

*

Back in his house, Michael woke up. The empty beer bottles littering his coffee table reminded him of the disaster of the day before. Also on the floor were old dvds that chronicled his once thriving career, now dead as the plant next to them.

When his phone rang, he grabbed it, seeing Tom's name, "The 'old' Mickey Quinlan here."

"Come on, Mick, it's not that bad."

"It seems much worse. After twenty years, I'm a roller skating joke?"

Tom's voice was firm, "It was Cecil Mercury. The guy literally and figuratively wears a cape."

"Was he really wearing a cape?" Michael was momentarily distracted from his pity party.

"He was. It was hard to miss."

"Do you know I was mistaken for Blake Greer's dad when I left that meeting? Don't tell me my career prospect isn't grim."

Tom pleaded, "Listen, Jim called and he said he and the students really need you back."

"Yeah, I got a text from him too," Michael sighed "I've got one more meeting to take." Ending the call, he scrolled through the pictures on his phone. Seeing a picture of Guinness, who seemed to smile into the camera cheered him. Another one was of Franny and Goliath. Then he played the video he took at the last dog obedience class.

Lauren instructed Guinness to wait for a toy that was just out of reach. "Wait is a command that means the dog can have it, just not yet."

It strengthened his resolve to get moving. He needed to see Jessica.

When she answered the door, Michael forced himself not to look shocked by her wan appearance, her scalp covered in a fashionable bandana.

They hugged and made small talk as she welcomed him into her home. He was relieved to see she seemed genuinely happy to see him. The young woman he remembered meeting only months ago now was wise and stoic.

"Everyone has scattered," Jessica sighed. "Maybe they think they'll catch it too. I've got cancer, not leprosy."

"Losing Kelly's friendship isn't much of a loss."

Jessica giggled, "Yeah, well I figured that out before I got sick. Did you know she wanted me to help her fake a stint in rehab?"

Michael shook his head and he told her about the chicken dinner fund-raisers in the small town where he'd been. She seemed delighted.

"I can't say I had a fund-raiser, but Joan brought over the hugest pot of chili I've ever seen. It was like if she could just bring me enough food, it would make the cancer go away."

Michael smiled at this. He was glad he didn't feel the need to fill the lag in conversation with inane chatter. Maybe he was learning something.

Jessica looked at him tenderly, "I'm glad you weren't scared to visit, Mickey."

"I was. That's why I'm here."

"Wow, when did you get cast as the decent guy?"

Michael shook his head, "It may be my final role."

Jessica took this in, "What's her name?"

Michael met her eyes and shook his head with a grin. "Once it appears on a tabloid, it's not going to matter. I'm at Kelly's mercy."

"Kelly got that part. She posted it today. However, she didn't mention you."

"Maybe being forgotten isn't so bad after all."

Jessica hesitated, then said, "By the way, I think someone beat Kelly to the punch of a tabloid picture. She posted one of you two at a restaurant yesterday. It's probably already on a tabloid."

"What?"

Chapter Twenty-five–The Greatest of These is Love

"As we come to the end of our training session, your dogs have made great progress," Lauren said as she looked over the class as they walked in a circle. "Can you think of anything that we're missing?"

The Bernese mountain dog lunged for the ramp, but the owner snapped him back into place. "Good job!" Lauren called. The owner of the Labrador said, "I don't know if we're missing anything. Toby's been great with only a few mistakes."

Lauren asked the group, "How do you all feel about your dogs now from when we started?" The response from the group made her smile. It was overwhelmingly positive. This is what she enjoyed so much, the bonding and progress.

"Don't forget that all these commands you've taught your dogs are great, but it's not the most important thing. Your dog will still make mistakes, just like you will. But you don't give up on your dog. The most important thing is you love and enjoy your dog, faults and all. Every relationship has its challenges, but surviving the good and the bad is what life's all about."

*

Lauren sat on her front porch sorting through her mail. More charity solicitations, an ALS newsletter (ugh), a letter from the bank. That last one was nothing she wanted to open. She looked at the tiny kitten sleeping in its cardboard box. It was already looking healthier.

Just then the sound of the UPS truck turning into her drive alerted both her and the dogs.

"Stay!" she ordered, then directed them quickly into the house. "Hi Jake," she greeted the friendly driver.

"Hey, Lauren, I didn't know you were living with someone," Jake handed her a thick manila envelope with Michael Quinlan written on the address.

"I'm not. Someone's renting the cabin, that's all." She took the envelope, noting the California address. As much as she wanted to believe that Michael receiving mail meant he would return, she didn't dare hope for it. It likely was the sender didn't hear of the change.

"Want me to give it to him?"

"Oh no, I'll let him have it." Lauren groused.

Jake gave her a peculiar look, which she fully deserved. However, she didn't feel like offering an explanation. She waved goodbye and returned to the porch, letting the dogs circle after the truck buzzed away.

Part of her wanted to rip open the envelope, since Michael apparently felt free to rifle through Tyler's things. However, she wouldn't stoop to that. And if she were honest, she wasn't sure how long she would resist snooping if she was bored and left alone with a box full of mysterious items. It wasn't like they were sealed shut, like this envelope. Besides, he told her the truth. It was hard to be fair and be angry at the same time.

Just when she thought she understood him, and that he understood her, he took off. Was he that incapable of commitment? Of course he was. Wasn't that his public track record? Did she really think she was fabulous enough to change that?

She threw the envelope onto her pile of mail. She decided to clean the cabin out, putting Michael's things in a box that she would close with duct tape. Later, she would ask Jim to give her a forwarding address. It seemed unlikely he would be back. While she was at it, she would clear out Tyler's things as well. It was time.

*

The fund-raiser for the local pet rescue group had finally arrived. Lauren was proud of her neighbors who began with simply rescuing some dogs out of the local dog pound. Using mostly foster homes for the dogs, their adoption rate rivaled much larger organizations.

When she and Tyler first married, they made fun of this little village, thinking they were destined to move somewhere significant. The option to move was there, but after visiting other areas of the country, they decided to stay put. The people may have lacked sophistication, but their hearts were huge. With the college nearby, the faculty and staff offered an eclectic mix. Once they opened the kennel, they were in it for good. Even now, when Lauren considered moving, she had a hard time imagining anywhere else would be as welcoming as tiny

Kettlesville.

She refused to think about how Michael had promised weeks ago he'd be here. As she walked into the village park, she grinned at the banner that read "Artists in the Dog House." She met Alice at the entrance and grabbed a brochure.

"They sure have a lot of entries this year," Alice said, admiring a dog house that looked like a log cabin.

Lauren shuddered as they examined an all pink dog house that seemed to have a Barbie theme. However, she smiled when she read that it was made by Sammy's father. Even dealing with his child's cancer, he made an effort to bring his child joy and help the organization at the same time.

"Which one are you going to bid on?" Lauren asked.

"Probably the winner. Which reminds me, what time do you have to be at the judge's table?"

Lauren cringed, "You know I get so much flack for whatever decision I make. The days of gracious losers seem far behind us."

Once she was equipped with her clipboard and donned her lariat with the judge badge, she did a more thorough exam of each house.

Alice meandered ahead of her, walking around a dog house painted to look like a barn. A large pink pig was on the side. "Hey, Lauren, are you achin' for some bacon?"

Lauren rolled her eyes, "This from the vegetarian?"

"Oh come on, that was funny." Alice laughed herself silly.

"I'm telling a story in my head, Alice," Lauren said, leaving her friend to her amusement.

The next dog house featured multiple entrances. She squatted down and crawled in for a better view. Suddenly, a face appeared at the opposite end.

"Michael!" Lauren screeched, hitting her head on the ceiling. As she backed out, Michael was there, rubbing her head, trying not to laugh without success. "You give me a headache, you know that?"

He apologized, then added, "I made a huge mistake."

Lauren continued rubbing the sore spot on her head, "What did you expect scaring me like that?"

"That's not what I meant. Leaving was a mistake."

"What was her name this time?" Lauren muttered, tapping the clipboard with her pen.

"Lauren."

Lauren snorted and turned away, "I'm kind of busy here."

As she moved on to another dog house, she sensed Michael fidgeting. Good, she hoped he was as confused as she was. She knelt down to examine the next model. Colorful, folk art-inspired decorations adorned it, with painted ceramic dog bowls sitting in the front entryway. She took out her water bottle and took a drink.

"Mind if I have a sip?"

Lauren stood back up, "I don't mind at all." She picked up

one of the ceramic dog bowls and poured water into it. "Here."

Michael took the proffered water bowl, raising an eyebrow at her, "Getting back into your good graces isn't going to be easy, is it?"

She tapped the bowl with her pen, "Lap it up, Honey." She turned to walk to the next entry, but her emotions rose quicker than she could think. She spun around and seethed, "Why did you leave?"

Her resolve to be stern melted when she saw Michael actually drinking from the bowl. Her hand went to her forehead. The man was a piece of work. This was the Michael Quinlan she always suspected existed; playful.

Michael set the dog bowl down and caught up with her, "I guess you could say it was about security."

"Job security?" When he shrugged, Lauren continued on into a people-sized dog house that was decorated like a cozy cottage.

Michael followed her, the two of them alone. "Acting has a shelf life."

Lauren relented, "So now what?" She leaned back on the wall next to an imitation fireplace.

Michael approached and stood right in front of her. He put an arm up, blocking her, "I've had some ideas."

Lauren decided to play along, leaning forward, saying coyly, "Really? I've had some too. Such as I don't think you should stay in the cabin anymore."

His expression showed he was hopeful, "The house?"

She ducked under his arm, "Yeah, the dog house." She tossed her head and headed for the door.

"Oh come on, Lauren," Michael pleaded, "Throw me a bone, will you?"

An oversized plastic bone sat by the door. Lauren picked it up and hurled it at him. He ducked, but it hit the hearth, making a resolute squeak.

*

The next day, Lauren looked out her window and noticed Michael by the kennel, raising a ladder by the broken downspout. She picked up the thick envelope to take to him. Before she opened the door, she watched him work. It was nice having him back, and not just because the downspout would finally be fixed. He sure looked good doing physical work. And she knew it was doing a world of good for him too.

On second thought, she tossed the envelope back on her desk, along with the other mail she chose to ignore, especially that pesky letter from the bank. She would give it to him later. No need to bother him when he was working.

As she walked over and stood at the base of the ladder watching him hammer, he stopped and looked down, "Thought I'd get your mind out of the gutter."

"Hahaha," Lauren crossed her arms, "You know comedy really isn't your thing after all." She watched a bit longer, feeling out of sorts, "And just so you know, this doesn't fix us either."

"Maybe we can talk after I come back from the final rehearsal?" Michael looked hopeful.

"Maybe," she turned to walk away, hearing Michael yelp as his hammer missed its target. Maybe it was wrong, but the sound of his pain made her smile.

Back in the house, she grinned to herself. She looked forward to talking to him. She looked again at the stack of mail. She had to quit putting it off and reached for the pile.

"Oh no!" Lauren stared at the letter from the bank. "This just can't be right."

*

Relief. It was the overriding emotion since returning. That and panic. It seemed Michael alternated between the polar opposites within minutes. If he thought of his career, the fear that his destiny as a voice-over for computer products took over. But if he looked outside the window of the little cabin, particularly in the direction of Lauren's farmhouse, he felt calm.

The final week of rehearsals for the college's productions was upon him. In the theater, he was invigorated.

As Jim instructed some students, Michael stood behind the curtain, making some notations in the script he carried.

Pam appeared and sidled up to him. Michael looked up and nodded, but in a moment, she leaned against him and breathed, "I've been meaning to ask you, what's a girl gotta do to get an audition?"

Before Michael could answer, Monty swooped in and

grabbed Pam's hand, "Hey! Leave my girlfriend alone!"

"I did not ask for that," Michael said, holding up his free hand.

"Sure, you show up here for easy action with college girls," Monty sniped. "Why don't you stick with that older woman?"

Monty turned, pulling Pam after him. Pam turned and gave him a wink. Michael felt sick, though he wasn't sure if it was the boldness of someone as young as Pam or the accusations of Monty that bothered him so much. However, he now realized who Kelly's informant was. It took him long enough, but it wasn't like he was a detective. Other things were on his mind, like trying to win Lauren's trust. It was amazing what others could do to quickly ruin his character, though over the years some of that was certainly his own fault.

After rehearsal, Michael and Jim chatted.

"It's a contemporary version of *She Stoops to Conquer*," Michael told him. "If I could get a part in that, I'd be thrilled."

"It's an intriguing concept," Jim commented. "How they update that story would be a challenge."

Just then Michael noticed Monty sneaking away. Whatever. How could he further hurt him?

"How are things going with Lauren?"

"She's listening to me, but I can tell she still isn't warming up at all," Michael said.

"Tom mentioned something to me about Kelly being upset. What happened?" Jim asked.

"The ruse Kelly used to lure me back was some promising script. Some pretentious director named Cecil Mercury was involved, which was the first red flag. I got out of it, but Kelly took the part. However, it was a bait and switch. It turned out to have a lot of lurid parts that were pretty sick even by Hollywood standards. Kelly was furious. She walked right off the set."

"It's easier to write trash than to be clever enough to keep it clean," Jim said.

Michael nodded at him, "You got that right."

"Tom said he barely recognizes your tone these days. Says you sound like a changed man."

Michael grinned and shrugged. He stood to leave, "Who knew I had to come to such a small place to expand my horizons?"

Chapter Twenty-six–True Love Chases Out Fear

While some kennel clients weren't prompt for their appointments, she knew this dog's owner was militaristic, and would never be late. That was an understatement.

Lauren tended her plants as Michael showed up. They were having civil conversations, which was progress. At least they were going to the play together.

As they chatted, the expected car pulled in front of the kennel door. The owner greeted Lauren, who stood to help the owner unload the food and dog bed. Then, the owner ordered, "Schatze, unload!"

A large Rottweiler stepped out of the car and walked directly to its owner. "Sit!" and the dog obeyed, still never letting its eyes move from the master's face. "Stay!" The dog owner carried the heavy food container to the front door. Michael would have stood to help, but this man was clearly in control of his dog and possibly everything else around him.

"Stand," the owner commanded. This time the dog stood and looked at Lauren, the faint hint of a tail wag in her direction.

"Schatze!" Tone was everything and this man seemed to yell instead of talk.

Lauren tried to intervene, "It's fine, let me take Schatze in for you."

"He took a step. Did you see that? Before I told him to come, he took a step. He's going to have to stay right there until I say it's okay for him to move."

Lauren bit her lip and glared at the man. "Mr. Hutchens, Schatze would rather die than disappoint you. I think he was just shifting his weight. Besides, I have an appointment out of town shortly. You wouldn't want me to be late would you?"

Mr. Hutchens' expression showed that being late was completely unacceptable. "I'm so sorry, Lauren. I sometimes forget you have a life outside of the kennel."

Lauren snorted, "Yeah, not much of one, but I do try to keep it going." She looked at the dog who was still frozen in its stance, awaiting his owner's word. Lauren again looked at the man, "May I?"

The man motioned his agreement.

"Schatze, come!" Lauren squealed in a happy voice. The dog bounded to her and through the door as she opened it.

Michael watched as the man gave him a polite salute before driving off.

When Lauren emerged and locked the kennel door, Michael asked, "What was that all about?"

He followed her as she headed into the house.

"His pride and joy is an obedient robot of a dog." Lauren sat, taking off her sneakers and slipping on sandals with a slight heel. "It makes me so sad that his dog obeys out of fear rather than love."

"It doesn't seem like that dog has much of a life."

Lauren grinned, "Actually, he does when he comes here. I don't ever go against an owner's wishes, but I must say I do for Schatze's sake. He didn't think his dog would be okay playing with the other dogs. But I tested him with my own."

"Why not?" Michael was still interested in the conversation, but was more interested in the way Lauren's legs looked when she stood and walked toward his car.

"Part of the guy's persona as a tough guy is wrapped up in his burly breed. He seems to think his dog is too aggressive to get along with the other dogs. But he's so wrong. That dog absolutely frolics. Do you know what he did once? I opened the door to the play area for him and Scout and Guinness. Schatze stopped at the door, then ran back to the basket of toys I keep in there. He took out a squeak toy and then raced out to join the other dogs. Now tell me that isn't a dog that needs to play. You can bet nothing as frivolous as a squeak toy is allowed in his world."

"You're pretty good to those dogs," Michael said as he steered out of the driveway.

"I just think a dog should be able to enjoy its life. I mean, life can be very hard. Why make it harder?"

Michael looked at her quickly, "And what about you? Are

you going to enjoy your life?"

Lauren looked at him, then back out of the front window. She was quiet for a long time. Finally she quipped, "I think we can enjoy our lives even when it is hard. It wouldn't be fair to say that Tyler and I didn't have lots of good times despite his illness. Sure, a lot of it was terrible. But we were still normal people who needed to laugh and have fun, even if it wasn't in the way we may have wanted. Sometimes I think I even forget that. There was joy mixed in with the sorrow."

"There's probably not many people who would admit that."

"No, it's easy to focus on the bad times. I know I have. But it's a lie to only remember the bad stuff. And I don't want to be a bitter person. My life isn't over and I intend to move forward and enjoy whatever lies ahead of me."

"Even though you're scared?" Michael asked, giving her a gentle poke with his elbow.

Lauren tried not to smile, but she did, still not taking her eyes off the road. "Yes, even though I'm scared. What about you?"

Michael wasn't ready for that. Could he honestly say he had the same amount of pluck? He grabbed her hand and gave it a squeeze, "Deal."

*

Lauren's enthusiasm was reserved, but Michael noticed that her argumentativeness was diminished. She put up no resistance to attending the theater's opening night when he asked her.

Jim stayed backstage, but Michael filed in with Alice and Lauren. He was pleased to see the crowd mostly dressed up. Lauren looked stunning. He noticed most eyes checking her out and ignoring him. If they looked at him at all, it was as if there was some vague register of familiarity, but not fully able to place where. Ah well, maybe that wasn't so bad. In general, fame had done him no favors. However, it was a drug he wasn't certain he could do without.

Franny bustled in, sitting by Michael with an excited expression. He was just glad she didn't sneak Goliath in by putting him in her giant handbag.

The curtain rose and the next two hours were riveting. When the students performed the grave side scene from *Our Town*, Monty was flawless as the grieving George. Pam, playing Emily watching the town mourn at her funeral, delivered her lines with gripping emotion.

"It goes so fast. We don't have time to look at one another."

Michael stole a glance at Lauren, who tearfully returned his look. He covertly put his hand over her shoulders, giving her a tender squeeze.

During the curtain call, the house erupted with applause. When Monty and Pam came on stage, the clapping was even more enthusiastic. Though Michael wasn't too keen on either of the actors as people, they weren't so different than how he was at their age. If only he could explain it to them. It wasn't fame as much as it was vanity that they craved.

Jim came on stage and took a bow as well. Then the whole cast pointed out to the audience. The spotlight landed on

Michael. He stood, graciously taking a quick bow before gesturing back to the stage. It was just a moment, but that familiar rush came back to him. It was a bit different from when he was on center stage, but it still felt good.

However, his ego took a beating shortly after while they filed out of the theater. He overheard a couple debating just who he was and what movie he was in, and they were unable to name one. The stinger was when the wife sighed, "Who knows? It was so long ago."

He deflated, wondering how quickly his work would disappear. Posterity was elusive. He was starting to understand Lauren's grief over losing a husband. How would his life be remembered?

*

Later Jim, Alice, Lauren, and Michael celebrated at the little diner. The farmers were even there, having attended the event. This time Franny did bring Goliath, though Raylene forbid the dog to actually enter the area where food was served. Instead, Raylene kept him in the pocket of her apron as she rung up customers.

Michael grinned at Lauren, "You know, maybe Raylene's not so bad after all."

Lauren nodded, "You're right. Maybe we should quit being grammar snobs."

"Never!" he grinned as they joined the others. Lauren made her way around the assembled group with a coffee pot until Michael took it from her, pouring as he went. Just as Michael felt a sense of peace fall on him, he noticed the look on Lauren's face as she stared at the door. The farmers quit talking and the diner quieted.

Kelly was in the house, and all her glittery, animal-printed-self let them know it.

One of the farmers muttered, "Did someone hire a stripper?"

Michael barely had time to set down the coffee pot before Kelly threw herself into him with a loud squeal of delight. He wondered if everyone else detected how contrived it sounded.

She breathlessly said, "Mickey, you can thank me for making your dream come true."

Another farmer looked at his buddy, "Yep, she's a stripper alright."

Kelly grabbed Michael and drug him to a booth, sitting down on the flat cushions. She recoiled, sprang up, delicately swatted the seat with a napkin and then sat back down. Removing a thick script from an envelope, she handed it to him like it was the Holy Grail.

And it was. "*She Stoops to Conquer?*" He whispered as he took it.

"Mickey Quinlan as Mr. Hardcastle," Kelly squealed.

He could hardly believe it. Then reality kicked in. He squinted at her, "What's your agenda here, Kelly?"

She held up her hands, all innocence, "No agenda, Mickey. I just want to apologize and make up for how much you've helped me."

He stared at the script as if he were in a trance. However, it was broken when one of the farmers asked for a refill. As he left the booth to fill the request, Kelly held up a laminated menu, using a napkin in each hand.

When Michael returned, she asked with disgust, "What? Is there a waitress strike in this town or something?"

"That was Merle. He had a knee replaced."

Kelly was befuddled, "So?"

"He needed help," Michael shrugged, as if she'd understand this elusive concept. "So what's the story with casting this?"

"I talked them into waiting for your answer. But you've got one more day, Mickey, and then…"

"Then what?"

Kelly simpered, "Then they're going to Blake Greer."

Michael was so stunned he barely registered Lauren's presence as she stood by their table.

Kelly whined, "Finally. About time we saw a waitress. Could you wipe my seat?" she flounced out of the booth and scooted in next to Michael, looping her arm through his.

Lauren put a hand on her hip, "I do enough of that in my day job."

"Oh, are you an au pair?" Kelly asked.

Before it could get uglier, Michael introduced them,

"Lauren, this is Kelly Smith."

"Fairbanks!" Kelly scolded him. "No wonder you didn't want that picture out there, Mickey. How embarrassing to be with a waitress."

Michael grimaced as Lauren asked, "Could I see you for a moment? 'Mickey'?" emphasizing his nickname.

He followed her to the other side of the restaurant, which wasn't far. The farmers watched them go from side to side like a tennis match.

"What's going on?" Lauren said.

He couldn't detect her mood from her tone, but he could guess. However, his excitement at the part was overwhelming. He explained it to her. "Just imagine what we saw tonight, but with an audience of millions instead of hundreds."

"Does a larger audience determine your significance?" She crossed her arms.

Tom joined them, "What's Kelly doing here?"

"She's got a script to *She Stoops to Conquer*. You know anything about this?"

"Sure. I sent you a copy over a week ago. Didn't you get it?"

"No." Michael heard Lauren make a funny sound.

She was pale. "You know anything about this?" He asked.

Lauren turned and left.

Lynne E. Scott

Chapter Twenty-seven–Strongest Evidence of Love Is . . .

Lauren watched the headlights of Michael's car as it drove down the lane from the cabin toward the road. It was dark, so he likely couldn't see that she was watching him pass before she stepped into the kennel. He wouldn't be back this time. She'd broken his trust.

Of all the ways she thought it would end with him, she never saw it coming back to her stupid mistake.

Tank loped out of his kennel run and greeted Lauren with a friendly nudge. She loved how mastiffs showed affection by swinging their backside into people. It nearly knocked her down, but she appreciated the gesture, "I'm glad you still like me. You're too big to have as an enemy."

After she let the dogs out and brought them back in for the night, she brought Tank into the training area. He still resisted following his owner's command. Lauren ran him around the circle, maybe she'd sleep better if she could work off her nervous energy. She also didn't want to think about Michael. Or anything.

"Sit." Tank sat.

"Down." Tank thought about it. Lauren held a treat at his nose and gradually moved it toward the ground and away from the dog's body. He slunk down and took the treat when Lauren praised him.

"Now, leave it." Lauren set another treat out about a foot from the dog's snout. Tank stared at the treat and at Lauren. She cocked her head to the side and folded her arms. When she didn't say anything for a couple minutes, Tank lowered his head between his paws and moaned.

"That's not so hard, now is it? Your reward is right there, no one's taking it," Lauren continued to stand still, sensing the dog struggling. This was a key moment. Tank wanted that treat. Lauren was expecting him to listen to her instead. She had to prove she had confidence in his abilities.

Calmly, Lauren walked to the treat and picked it up and turned her back to the dog. She glanced behind her, only to see Tank's ears perked, but he hadn't moved a muscle. She continued across the room then turned.

"Tank, come!" The dog pushed himself up with some effort and trotted toward her, tail wagging. Lauren laughed and patted his head, "Good job! That was hard, wasn't it?" Lauren hugged the dog to her and patted his back side, "Now, that was sacrifice!"

*

Later that day, Lauren tried to relax in the hammock. It was difficult when her thoughts were a jumble. She tugged Tyler's shirt tighter around her, closing her eyes. Of all the strange emotions she'd experienced since meeting Michael, the one she couldn't escape at this moment was abandonment. She felt completely alone.

The sound of her dogs gnawing on their toy bones grated on her nerves. She could hear a cat or two walking along the banister of the porch, one performing its grooming ritual.

"Mew."

The dogs stopped chewing. The cats stopped licking. Lauren sat up, pointing straight at the dogs, "Don't move! Stay!"

She swooped over to pick up a cat in each arm and herded the dogs inside. Following the sound of the tiny mew, Lauren dreaded what she would find. Right now she was at her cat capacity. How would she afford one more vet bill for shots and fixing a cat?

Still, she tromped down the steps, creeping closer to the sound of the mews. Using the universal language of cats, she softly called, "Here kitty-kitty-kitty."

A tiny ball of steel gray fluff bounded over to her. Lauren noted it came from near the road, where it likely was tossed from the car. Kneeling down, Lauren swept the kitten into her arms, standing up to cuddle it.

The kitten's purr seemed to fill the air. Examining it, Lauren noted it was covered with fleas. Plus, it was shaking, probably from hunger. It didn't look old enough to be away from its mother.

The dogs bounded out of the house to investigate as did the cats as soon as Lauren opened the door. She happily shut them outside as she took the tiny kitten to the sink. There she ran the water in a small stream until it was warm. The kitten was so exhausted it didn't put up any fight as Lauren gently washed it. The water turned brown after flowing over the kitten as the filth came off.

"Look, you fit right in the palm of my hand," she whispered. The kitten peered up at her, helpless. "You'll be clean soon."

After she finished, she wrapped the kitten in an old kitchen towel and held it close to her body, warming it. "You're so tiny." The purrs started again and Lauren was struck at how completely vulnerable it was. She walked out on the back porch where her menagerie of animals were preoccupied with other ventures.

As Lauren looked at the sky, she thought of herself in the big universe, much like this tiny cat. "I lay my life in the palm of Your hand," she said. Looking down at the kitten, she noticed its eyes were closed, sound asleep. Lauren wondered how it could so easily trust her, a complete stranger.

*

Michael took long strides through the airport. He was angry. For all her talk about being honorable, Lauren still betrayed him. She now joined the ranks of everyone else who used him. Irritation overruled common sense in his life. Again.

This little fact crept into his mind as Kelly ranted on, her arm looped through his, "I've got so much work to do for my part. I'll make a beautiful princess, don't you think, Mickey?"

"You've got a film starting too?"

Before she could answer, he recognized a loud housedress.

Walking to her, "Franny, what are you doing here?"

"Going to see my grandson." Franny chortled, "Do you think you could make an autograph for him? He's a big fan."

"Sure," Michael said, kneeling and taking the pen she found in one of her many pockets, "I didn't know I had any left."

He glanced over his shoulder and noticed Kelly shifting her weight side to side. She looked around, hoping no one noticed her proximity to the strange woman.

Franny patted his arm after he handed her the signed paper and pen, "After my son died, my grandson and I watched your funny movies. Oh, we laughed and laughed. They brought us so much joy. I didn't know you were the same guy until last night at the theater."

"You made my day, Franny," Michael kissed her cheek.

"Mickey, we're almost to our gate," Kelly said impatiently.

Franny peered around his shoulder, "Who does Miss Fancy think she is?"

Michael turned around and looked at Kelly, then back at Franny, "I have no idea."

Reluctantly he joined Kelly and hurried for the gate. Kelly clucked, "What a total loser. How you ever managed to hang out with those hill jacks is beyond me. But," she shrugged, "I suppose slumming it with the rednecks may come in handy for some future role for you."

"What did you say?" Michael froze. How could he be so stupid? He should know better than to listen to Kelly. Shouldn't it be the other way around? Not so long ago, it was.

"Seriously? What can they do for you?"

Michael stood still, "Sometimes it's about doing for someone else."

Kelly walked forward, "Oh please. First class is boarding. Hurry up."

Michael let his bag slip off his shoulder.

Kelly made an exasperated sound and stomped her foot again. "Don't do this to me!"

"To you?" Michael quizzed, "What exactly am I doing to you?"

"I can't be Lady Hardcastle if you're not going to be Captain Hardcastle," she blurted.

"Ah," Michael said, picking up his bag. "I see how it is. The deal is off for me. Good luck with you and Blake Greer."

"But Mickey!" Kelly stamped her foot and whined. It was quite a performance.

"You know Kelly, you have what it takes to be successful. Good luck." Michael headed for the bar in the first class lounge. He sat in front of the airport windows, watching the planes land and take off. It was getting dark. He took out his phone and scrolled through his contacts. He deleted Cecil Mercury. He deleted Kelly. He came to Lauren's name. He couldn't delete it. But he couldn't call her either.

He sipped his drink and looked out the window, thinking of

the song Lauren sang with that little girl. "Fly away Jack. Fly away Jill."

*

Perhaps Lauren should have cancelled the obedience class the next day. Her mood was surly at best. From experience, she knew patience when dealing with both people and canines was important. She gritted her teeth and got through the lesson.

It didn't help that the topic was about different dog personalities. "Beware of the conniving dog," she said. "They'll watch you all day, waiting for an opportunity to get what they want. Don't leave yourselves—or your dinner—vulnerable to their ways."

After class was over and everyone left, she went outside and noticed a loose spot on the kennel downspout. How she hated that thing. It was like it taunted her helplessness. She dropped the stack of dirty dog bowls she was carrying, reached high, and grabbed it. It hardly moved. Frustrated, she lifted up her legs, letting her full weight drag the spout down. She dropped to the ground when it finally gave way.

"Ha!" Lauren yelled with triumph.

"Uh, Lauren?"

Lauren turned to see Wendy and Carly staring at her. Great. What kind of new level of hell had she discovered? These two were the last she could handle with her now spent patience. It seemed they'd gone from friends to judges to enemies to her.

"We brought you a little something," Wendy said, pulling Lauren up.

Wendy handed her a large colorful gift bag, "I just finished it for you."

Lauren accepted the bag, removing an elaborately decorated album. "What is this for?"

"Open it," Wendy said.

In it were pictures of her and Tyler, which was wonderful since she had virtually none of the two of them together. Another was a charming shot of Tyler hugging Franny, who looked delighted. She felt a lump rise in her throat when she turned a page and saw one of Tyler carrying her, a bandage around her ankle. It was so long ago, Lauren nearly forgot.

"You two shouldn't have," Lauren said softly. "But I'm glad you did."

"Here," Carly handed her a smaller album, "But this one you have to finish."

Lauren looked at the two smiling women. She felt completely off center. Inside the smaller album were pictures of her and Michael, from the fair, the fund-raiser, and the theater premiere. In the back were pages to be filled.

"Oh, I don't know if there will be any more," Lauren said stoically. "But I appreciate what you're telling me."

The three women exchanged embraces and tears. But they were the best kind of tears. The kind that heal.

*

Lauren sat in the diner, toying with her coffee mug. It barely registered when it was filled. She absently said, "Thanks,

Raylene."

She startled when a male voice responded, "You're welcome."

"Michael!" she said with a smile, until she remembered she was mad at him.

"Ha! I saw that! You were happy to see me. I caught you!"

He sat while she uncomfortably shifted in her seat.

Both of them heard the farmers whispering from across the diner. One mumbled, "This is better'n that world poker tournament on television."

Michael folded his hands on the table and exhaled slowly, "I've made a decision. Or maybe it's an un-decision."

"I'm un-listening," Lauren said.

"What does that mean?"

Lauren looked down, "There's always going to be something more interesting than me."

Michael shook his head and put his hand on her arm, giving it a slight squeeze. "Trust me, there are few things, or people, more interesting than you or this little town of yours."

"Well," she said, "It's not mine. Not yet."

The air conditioning blower kicked on, causing Lauren to rub her arms and elbows. Michael slid off the cushions and onto her side of the booth. He unbuttoned his long-sleeved shirt and rested it over her shoulders.

"We're a quaint bunch, aren't we?" She smiled at him, though it didn't quite reach her eyes.

"I've always loved quaint."

"This isn't a laboratory for you to do research, you know," she pulled his shirt tighter over her shoulders. "We're people with feelings. Yes, there are varying degrees of intelligence and a poor command of grammar. This odd place, with authentic and flawed people, is my home."

"Look, I know I left. Again," Michael said quietly. "But you didn't give me that script."

Lauren sighed. "I know. I was going to. Would you believe me if I said I forgot? There was kind of a lot going on."

The farmers were mesmerized. Their whispers were getting under Lauren's skin. "Could you move back to your side, please?"

He did, but reached for her hand, "I don't have it all figured out yet, okay? It's not that easy to just start over."

"Really? Everyone tells me it is." She drained her coffee, stood and said, "Let me know when your visit is over. I'm looking forward to cleaning up the trash." Only when she got in her truck did she realize she was still wearing his shirt.

Chapter Twenty-eight–Come

"I'd like to try to put Goliath through that Canine Good Citizen test. Maybe I can get him into one of those therapy programs at the nursing home."

"That's a great idea, Franny," Lauren was pleased that Franny was spreading her generosity in non-casserole ways. "You and Goliath are really making some good progress. I'm proud of you."

Franny sighed, "I'm still having trouble with him coming to me."

" 'Come' is the hardest command for a dog to consistently follow. Everything is more interesting than listening to their owner. And you can't scold him when he comes, he has to feel safe to come to you." Lauren patted her arm, "But act as if he will listen to you. Keep your expectations high. Most likely, he'll rise to meet them."

*

After another sleepless night, Lauren crawled downstairs. She forced herself to head to the kennel. The downspout was fixed. That was weird. Maybe she was dreaming. After finishing her kennel duties, something niggled the back of her mind. Once back inside the house, she saw the stack of mail, including the envelope still waiting to be delivered to Michael.

Grabbing the pile, she began to sort it, finally opening the envelope from the bank. She gasped. Foreclosure. How could this be? She'd made the one payment. When was that? Normally she didn't let important things slip. She'd just been so distracted.

It was time to pull her act together. She noticed something in the kitchen to take as a token of apology. She really had blown it with the envelope, she realized that. She picked it up, along with the envelope and called Guinness and Scout and headed for the cabin. She walked quickly, hoping he was still sleeping. Fortunately, there was no stirring and she quickly slipped both items between the screen door and made a hasty retreat.

Guinness scooped up a ball and jabbed it at Lauren's leg. She reached down and threw it for him. "Now I'm good enough to play with you, huh?" Guinness raced after it, grabbed it. He hesitated when he was almost back to her. His ears twitched and he ran over to the cabin, sniffing around the door. "Looking for someone better than me, huh?" she moped. Scout followed her, but Guinness lagged behind. Traitor.

Her day didn't promise to get much better. She anticipated a long day of bank visits and phone calls.

*

On his way over to the theater, Michael opened the door and almost tripped over a pineapple. He picked it up and grinned. Then he noticed the tattered envelope. He slipped the script out and looked at it. Then, he tossed it in the trash.

He walked down the hallway, meeting Jim along the way. "Tom called. Pam got that part."

Michael grinned, "Kelly got shut out by a younger woman. Now there's some poetic justice. Now where am I going?"

"It's right down here," Jim led the way.

Michael stopped at the door, admiring the shiny nameplate on the door. "I've spent most of my life avoiding offices. Now I have my own. This is hard to believe."

He walked in, putting a satchel on the chair behind the desk. "I'm not sure I can sit behind one of these," he said, shaking his head at Jim.

"Look again," Jim said, pointing to a frame on the desk.

Michael picked it up. It was a picture of Lauren at the Pork Rind Festival. He sat down, trying the chair's wheels as he pushed it back and forth. "Maybe I can."

*

A week later, Lauren steeled herself for what promised to be an even worse appointment. With only her semi-loyal dogs by her side, she walked over to the cabin and knocked on the door.

When Michael opened the door, he ignored her stern expression and pulled her in by the arm. His enthusiasm made it hard to remain somber.

"I was hoping you'd come over." He led her to the table and

poured her some coffee.

"No, Michael, don't be nice to me," Lauren looked out the back door. "You have to move out."

Michael sat at the table and took a long sip, "No, I don't."

"I'm not playing a game with you. The bank owns this cabin now. I had to do it." She turned back to the window as tears welled in her eyes.

"No," Michael started.

Lauren held up her hand, closing her eyes. "It's over."

"My visit is," Michael said.

Lauren sat and took a deep breath. "If you're going to leave, then I'm going to tell you the truth. I didn't intentionally forget to give you that envelope. It got thrown into a pile of mail I should have been paying attention to. Story of my life."

Michael looked remarkably calm, "It worked out for the best anyway."

"Maybe from your perspective," Lauren sighed.

"My perspective has changed considerably," Michael leaned forward. "When I got here, my attitude was pretty arrogant. I didn't trust anyone. I was cautious, prepared for someone to use me. Normally, I'd just use them first, if I must."

Lauren looked up and shook her head, "You didn't use me. At least I don't think you did."

"You attracted me. You . . . your essence. Not what you could do for my career or how you would look next to me in a picture."

"Well, I have taken you around town and introduced you to the movers and shakers," she smirked.

He put his hand over hers. "Lauren, I'm not proud of leaving you behind—not once, but twice. You changed everything for me."

She looked away from his intense gaze, "Glad I could help."

"That's it? I don't mean that in a 'thank you, Life Coach' kind of way. I mean it in that you've made me into a better man," he cupped her chin in his hand and raised her eyes to meet his. "That's why I said I'm not moving."

Lauren's brow furrowed. "Oh, well, you're going to have to move out of here." Lauren struggled to keep her composure. "You wouldn't want to stay in this dinky place anyway."

He walked away, retrieved a piece of paper, and then handed it to her. She couldn't believe it. It was the deed to the cabin. She struggled against the hope that swelled in her heart. With a cry of joy, Lauren threw herself into his arms. Michael swung her in a small circle, which caused the dog to leap and bark.

When Michael set her down, he held her face in his hands, wiping her tears with his thumbs.

Lauren shook her head, "I can't believe it. You've decided to—"

"Stay."

A WORD FROM THE AUTHOR

While this story is a work of fiction, and its resemblance to any person or situation is purely a coincidence, many people may wonder if it is "my" story. While it's true that I have had a boarding kennel business for many years, and I did have a husband who died of ALS, the story of Lauren, Tyler and Michael are truly their own. Because ALS gets little attention as an "orphan disease," I wanted to keep that particular aspect similar. Lauren was deliberately given challenges and struggles different from my own.

However, it's also true that I once chased a pig down the road. And it really took several highly educated women to trap it in the bushes around my house. Also, a clerk in a now-closed tiny grocery store really did ask me what red onions look like. You just can't make that stuff up.

"I don't need a fantasy life as once I did.
That is the life of the imagination that I had a great need for.
Films were the perfect means for satisfying that need."
Olivia DeHavilland

ACKNOWLEDGMENTS

Truly the scope of people who helped with this story can't truly be thanked enough. This story began as the first screen play I wrote in 2004. It has changed numerous times since then, with many eyes upon it offering suggestions to strengthen and focus the story. Even though I have much in common with Lauren, I've learned a lot in the years since I first gave Lauren her personality and challenges. While I didn't want to change too many of her hard edges or give her the "wisdom of years," I hope the story as a whole can offer more clarity to those who find themselves in impossible pain.

A partial list of readers/editors include Marilyn Nelson, Trina Nelson Thomas, Ruth Johnson, Sue Fitzgerald and Darlene Bowers. Numerous others were forced to read early drafts of the script that I happily forced upon anyone who asked….my apologies and thanks.

A special thank you to Darlene Bowers whose talent produces both beauty and professionalism in all she does. She prepared this document (and other drafts) as well as polishing the formatting.

Cover artwork by Ellie Miller

ABOUT THE AUTHOR

Lynne Scott began writing with the craft of screenwriting and has completed five screen plays. NANOWRIMO challenged Lynne to try her hand at novel writing. Since 2009, she has completed several novels and one novella. Her first published work is "Dingo Devotionals: Learning to Heel."

Lynne began Good Shepherd Boarding Kennel in 1998 and has continued it for seventeen years (and counting). Lynne also became a licensed Zumba instructor in 2011.